LOS ANGELES

ALSO BY CAMERON WALKER

National Monuments of the U.S.A.

*Points of Light: Curious Essays on Science, Nature,
and Other Wonders Along the Pacific Coast*

HOW TO CAPTURE CARBON

HOW TO CAPTURE CARBON

STORIES

CAMERON WALKER

LOS ANGELES

Library of Congress Cataloging-in-Publication Data

Names: Walker, Cameron (Writer), author.
Title: How to capture carbon : stories / Cameron Walker.
Other titles: How to capture carbon (Compilation)
Description: Los Angeles : What Books Press, 2024. | Summary: "In a dozen
   radiant stories, award-winning author Cameron Walker brings readers to
   the water's edge, where the known world collides with magic and with the
   mysterious depths of the human heart. Here, a pandemic turns children
   into sea creatures, a woman bakes unusual pie crusts after a natural
   disaster, and a young man sets off to see the world in a flying coat. Lyrical
   and dreamlike, How to Capture Carbon navigates the seas of a changing
   climate and the transformative power of loss--and of love."-- Provided
   by publisher.
Identifiers: LCCN 2024018203 | ISBN 9798990014947 (trade paperback)
Subjects: LCGFT: Short stories.
Classification: LCC PS3623.A35883 H69 2024 | DDC 813/.6--dc23/eng/20240521
LC record available at https://lccn.loc.gov/2024018203

Cover art: Gronk, *I've Always Loved Rumi*, mixed media on paper, 2022,
reprinted with permission from *The Stranger You Are*,
art by Gronk and poetry by Gail Wronsky (Tia Chucha, 2022).

Book design by Ash Good, www.ashgood.com

What Books Press
363 South Topanga Canyon Boulevard
Topanga, CA 90290

WHATBOOKSPRESS.COM

for Chris

STORIES

STAR, FISH

THE VOICES OF THE TEACHERS come through the computer speakers: each child must pick a project. My oldest son picks the state of Oregon. My middle son draws pictures of mythological creatures: a Minotaur, a Pegasus, a dragon. My youngest son is not yet in school, so he picks flowers out of the flower bed and replants them back in the same soil. "More flowers, Mama," he says.

I pick a project too. I decide to study starfish. There is a tattoo of a starfish on the inside of my left wrist. I got it when my brother disappeared. "They're called sea stars," my oldest son says. "They're not fish, they're echinoderms."

Echinoderms. I look it up online. These include sea stars, brittle stars, sand dollars, sea urchins, and crinoids. I look up crinoids. There are two kinds: feather stars and sea lilies. My sons say they would like a snack. I find a knife and cut an apple into thin slices. I arrange the slices around the edge of a plate and put grilled cheese sandwiches in the middle.

When my children ask about my brother, I tell them he was a marine biologist. He went to distant research stations with names like flowers: Kaikoura, Moorea. I show my sons on a map.

Each day of the quarantine my boys become slightly less human. We are at home avoiding a virus that turns people's lungs into liquid. Instead my children are turning into sea creatures, as the sea is the only place it is safe to go. We walk there every morning and the dark green water pulls at my throat like a magnet. It seems to be pulling, too, on the saltwater deep within my sons' cells.

At the beach, I find a stick and draw labyrinths in the sand. At first my sons are interested in following the path, but then they realize that the way in is the same as the way out. They stand at the water's edge and let the sea lick at their toes.

My oldest son writes that Oregon is a place with beautiful trees and an interesting history. He has been there once and remembers nothing except that we watched movies in the car. We do not know when we can travel again, so instead I show the boys the postcards that my brother sent me from all over the world. On a postcard from Tahiti, there is a photo of a flower that looks like an open hand. On the other side, there is a printed caption: *Legend has it that the tiare apetahi is the hand of a girl who believed her true love would never return. At the top of the sacred mountain, she broke off her arm and planted it in the earth to represent her love. Then, overcome with sorrow, she threw herself from the mountain. People have tried to grow the flower elsewhere, but these attempts have been unsuccessful. Fewer than 100 flowers remain.*

I do not show my sons what my brother wrote. He had scrawled scientific names and a series of numbers on the back, as if he had been taking notes instead of writing to me.

Climate change may be good for feather stars. One scientist finds that feather stars regenerate their arms more quickly as the water warms. Another scientist argues that if coral reefs die, the feather stars will vanish, too. Feather stars are 200 million years old. After a day when everyone works on their projects, I feel even older.

My oldest son grows small, pale-blue tentacles above his upper lip like a mustache. My middle son, the artist, begins collecting colorful things—marbles, strands of yarn, LEGO pieces. He glues the things he finds to his back, which seems to have grown rounded and hard. My youngest son looks for more flowers to cut and replant. He has taken everything our garden has grown.

Perhaps I should be worried, but I can't stop watching videos of the feather stars. They are like a dozen windmills made of eiderdown, each circling and falling and rising through the water. My oldest son tells me it is not screen time any more. He says he wants a snack. I pour different cereals into tiny bowls and arrange them on the table in concentric circles.

Sea lilies look like feather stars, but they have a stalk like a flower that connects them to the substrate. They can move on their stalks—usually slowly, but one video caught a sea lily running at 140 meters an hour. That is how long it can take my youngest son and I to walk around the block. When I walk, I feel as if I am dragging my own stalk through heavy water. But when I look down, I find I still have two feet, skin and muscle, ligament and bone.

We walk to the beach again. If we go early we see hardly anyone else. A good thing, because people have started wearing masks and it frightens my sons to see people who are only bodies and eyes. It might frighten people more to see my sons. The youngest is sprouting new, feathery limbs from his shoulders.

My boys walk alongside each other. Often they fight, but sometimes they take each other's hands and step into the water, my youngest looking at the older boys as if they were twin suns. I remember when my brother and I were like this. He was the big one, I was small, and I looked at him the same way. My heart squeezes in on itself. I draw the lines of another labyrinth and place a round, flat rock at its center.

"Starfish are brutal," my brother told me once. "They stick their stomachs out through their mouths. They can pry open clams and dissolve the insides into digestive goo." My parents still talk about my brother when I call them in Florida. He was the oldest, he glowed with promise. My father still knows the names of the species my brother studied. *Pycnopodia helianthoides*, the sunflower star, slowly dying along the Pacific coast. *Acanthaster planci*, the crown-of-thorns, destroyer of coral reefs. *Stichaster australis*, a keystone species that holds its ecosystem together.

My parents don't know all the other things my brother studied, the ones that studied him back. *Flunitrazepam, methamphetamine.* They believe he is still on an expedition, that when my brother returns he will bring something marvelous and strange. My parents' faces blur and stutter on the video chat. They do not ask to talk to my children, and for once, I am relieved. I do not want them to see what I have let my boys become.

When I was young, I used to lie awake long past my bedtime until my brother was done with his lab reports, his intricate diagrams of algae. We would climb out through his bedroom window and onto the roof. We looked at the constellations and talked about the future. My brother wanted to be a famous marine biologist, like Jacques Cousteau except not French. I wanted to be an astronaut. We could sometimes see the space shuttle launch from where we lived in St. Augustine. As the shuttle glowed and then disappeared into the sky, I wished that someday, I would be going with it.

Now I am a mother and he is almost certainly dead. I imagine him drowning in crystal-blue water. I imagine his own stomach swallowing him after it grew tired of what he was feeding it.

The virus spreads, both around us and within. My oldest child is the one that stays most human. So many tentacles, but still he has arms and legs and a mouth. He asks for a snack. I make an egg white. Then I make another egg white, and two more fried eggs for his brothers. I try to get each yolk perfectly in the middle, but every time I flip the egg, the yolk slips off center and runs across the skillet.

Now I have to haul the youngest boy to the beach in the wagon because his feathery limbs no longer support him on land. I draw a big labyrinth on the sand and my middle son clatters through it, sideways. He cuts a piece of yarn neatly off his back with the larger of his two claws. I follow the yarn and find that he has shed his entire shell and left it in the center. When I look again, he inhabits an even larger shell, this one iridescent, protecting all his softness. It is better than a mask: I can't even see his eyes.

At home I take out the last postcard I got from my brother. I have never shown the boys this one. My brother scribbled over both sides of the card, his writing even covering the photo of a beach somewhere in Bali. The writing is in a language I do not recognize. The only familiar part is my address.

I trace the sea star on the inside of my wrist. My brother always could see the smallest fissures in me, the ones that no one else could. A few words from him could be the edge of a lever, fracturing the world I thought I'd made. When he disappeared, there was no one left who could break me.

At first I was relieved. Now I miss how well he saw me more than anything—more than teachers in their real classrooms with my children, more than a world where everyone has faces and can hold each other by the hand.

When the boys ask for a snack, the only way I recognize them is by their hunger. I see the knife on the kitchen counter, ready to cut an apple into slices, a carrot into sticks. The silver blade makes me shiver, but I know what I need to do.

My oldest son binds up the wound. "The capital of Oregon is Salem," he tells me. My middle son finds a picture of Medusa. He puts a crayon into his claw and writes "Mom" on the picture.

He adds a crooked heart. They watch while I plant my hand in the garden. My tattoo disappears under the dirt.

Then they ask for a snack. I press a jar of peanut butter against my ribs with my bandaged arm and open the lid with my right hand. I arrange crackers on a plate and place a spoonful of peanut butter on each one. Outside, the tips of my planted fingers reach toward the sun.

When my flower grows bigger, I take it down to the water. At my wedding, I stood at the edge of another ocean with a rose. I tossed it into the water to remember all those who weren't there with us: my grandfather, my new husband's mother, a few beloved friends. My brother had flown in from the South Pacific. His skin was the warbled texture of coral, his breath sweet with rum. It was the last time I ever saw him.

This time, when the flower of my hand floats out to sea, my children follow. The sun reflects so relentlessly off the waves that it is hard to even see their outlines. For a moment, I imagine the world if my children had never been, and whether the things I had lost—my left hand, my brother, what I thought was my life—would reappear to take their place.

I miss my brother so much. I call his name without thinking.

And then I can't stop. I call the names of the sea stars, the names of the drugs. The names I gave my sons before they were born. The names I gave them when they emerged from the watery world inside me. The names of the creatures they are now, anemone and decorator crab and feather star. I step into the water, soaking my running shoes, my yoga pants, the thin shirt from a concert I went to twenty years ago. I have been wearing these clothes so long that I no longer recognize myself, that I no longer would know my own name if the sea gave it back to me. The water swirls around my empty wrist.

Then my sons, my creatures, surround me. Their claws, their tentacles, their hands, caress the stump at the end of my arm. Do sea stars tingle like this when they feel a limb go missing? Is there somewhere that the vanished part still exists, even when something new grows to take its place?

My hand does not reappear. But my children do. My youngest son rests his face against my belly and there is no brush of feathers, only skin. "You went swimming in your clothes," he says. "I want to do that, too." He is still a child after all, with pajama bottoms and sleep-matted hair.

At home, my sons take photos of their projects and upload the photos to their online classrooms. The teachers give each project a tiny image of a heart. My middle son sheds his last shell and reorganizes his art supplies. My oldest son's eyes are round and watchful, like you always are after something has changed you.

My youngest son asks me to take a picture of the flowers he has replanted in the garden. "More cheese, Mama," he says. "Now give me a heart for my photo, like my brothers." I touch my fingertip to the image of the empty heart on the screen, and it fills up. Together, my son and I water the flowers. He looks longingly at my other hand.

ADULT SWIM

THE LIFEGUARD'S WHISTLE BLEW: time for adult swim. Ruby dragged her herself and her favorite polka-dot swimsuit up the steps at the corner of the pool. She didn't want to get out, not today, the first time her mother had been back to the pool since the baby had disappeared.

"Go on," her mother said. Her mother hadn't played with her at all today, just sat at the edge of the pool with her feet dangling into the water. When she'd tried to coax her mother in, her mother had said that Ruby was six, which meant she was old enough to play on her own. Even now, as Ruby stood on the top step, her mother was watching the sky. Ruby looked up, too. Nothing but two small clouds.

Suddenly, the air seemed to cool down around her. Ruby looked at her mother: her mother's sky-bleached eyes narrowed. Maybe her mother knew something about the clouds. A storm was coming, that was it. Ruby sighed and got all the way out of the pool. A storm coming, and she was getting hungry, too.

Her mother pulled on a swim cap and goggles, then slid into the water and under the line of buoys that marked the deep end of the pool, a place that Ruby had never been. In the deep end, the bottom of the pool sloped down and away and made Ruby's stomach churn. This was what she hated the most: being left alone on the hot pool deck while her mother's white cap sailed off to the far side of the pool.

Ruby lay face-down on the deck. Little chips of sparkly stone in the cement glared at her like a thousand little eyes. A bee circled her head. She was very still.

She wanted to get to her mother, but her mother had told Ruby not to move, or else. There were so many things *or else* could mean. When the bee moved on, Ruby wrote the words on the pool deck with a wet fingertip. *Or else.*

It was almost pretty with the watery letters running together. *Orelse.* A fairytale name. That's what they could name the next baby. Ruby would tell her mother about it when she stopped swimming.

Her mother hadn't picked out a name for the lost baby. Even before it vanished—Ruby wasn't quite sure how the baby had gotten away, or why no one looked for it still—Ruby's mother slept all the time. Her father, banished to the waking world with Ruby, told clumsy bedtime stories which never seemed on the verge of coming true like her mother's did.

Orelse. Ruby wanted to tell her mother before she forgot. *Before I forget*—that was another thing her mother always said. And *wait* and *stop* and *don't touch.* So many don'ts: *don't run, don't come in here with all that dirt, don't swim after you eat.* Why not? Ruby had always wondered. *Orelse*, her mother always said.

Ruby pressed herself up and went to sit at the side of the pool to tell her mother about the name. The imprint of her wet suit on the cement began to vanish. But her mother didn't stop swimming to listen, even when Ruby put her feet in the pool and kicked to make the biggest splashes she could. The lifeguard blew a short note on his whistle. "All the way out," the lifeguard said.

Ruby remembered she was hungry and took her feet out of the water. People were picnicking on the nearby grass. Ruby edged toward one family that had a cooler full of watermelon. "Hello," the woman said. "Would you like some watermelon? It's okay with your mom?" Ruby nodded.

She ate the slice the woman gave her, and stood there until the woman handed her another and another. "My, you're hungry, aren't you? Swimming does that."

"Thank you," Ruby said. She returned to the deck and lay down on her full stomach. Bees circled again and Ruby went still so they would not notice her.

Finally, the whistle blew. "Free swim," the lifeguard called.

Her mother came up beside Ruby and shook her wet body like a dog's, spraying Ruby. Ruby squealed. Her mother giggled, a sound Ruby hadn't heard in weeks. Her mother squatted next to her and wiped drops of water from Ruby's face with her gentle thumb. Then, harder, at the corner of Ruby's mouth. "You haven't eaten anything, have you?" She took hold of Ruby's wrist. The goggles had left raw marks like a second pair of eyes on her mother's face

"I haven't," Ruby said.

"Really?" She looked around where Ruby had been lying and then over at the picnic lawn. Ruby felt her mother's fingers loosen.

"Mama?" Her mother, watching the families on the grass, didn't answer. There she went again, somewhere Ruby couldn't reach.

Ruby pulled her wrist from her mother's fingers and threw herself into the pool. The lifeguard shook his head at her when she came up for air. His mouth shaped the words "No running."

At the side of the pool, Ruby gripped the concrete edge with her fingers and climbed hand-over-hand along the wall to the buoys that separated the deep end from the shallow. Her mother had her eyes closed, her face pointed to the sun. Ruby closed her eyes, too, and went under.

On the far side of the rope, everything felt different: the water bluer, colder. Ruby's stomach swirled. She looked again for her mother. There she was, squinting at Ruby, the red marks around her eyes fading. Her mother lifted her arm and waved.

Ruby felt her stomach start to expand. She leaned back into the water, hands on her belly. Floating felt so easy now with this fullness inside. The water cradled her, gurgling in her ears. A small breeze passed over. Everything around her moved, but inside she felt still, complete.

Her stomach kept growing. Now the size of melon, now a pumpkin, a beach ball. Her belly rolled her forward, lifted her above the water's surface. Her suit's polka dots became small suns.

Was this what her mother knew would happen? Ruby peered down over her new self. Her mother was at the edge of the pool, her arms reaching out to Ruby, her mouth open.

"I'm sorry, Mama," Ruby called down. "I ate some watermelon." Her mother was so far away now. The girl patted her belly, feeling the warmth of her hand on what was growing inside. "It's okay, Mama. I thought of a name for the baby. You're going to love it. It's just the kind of thing you would love."

RIPENING

MY SISTER ALWAYS LOOKED even more beautiful when she ate. Maybe this was why my father preferred her, something I first noticed as we drove back from camping in Montana, when I was nine and Lila was fourteen. Our parents had bought a flat of cherries at a roadside stand. Lila and I spit the pits at each other across the back seat. Then my mother showed us how to tie the stems into knots with our tongues.

My mother always had a certain kind of magic. I wonder now what would have happened had she taught Lila something else. Something that could have protected her from my father.

The red marks at the corners of Lila's lips turned her smile into a cluster of fallen petals. She was ripe, irresistible. Eventually I stood on the backseat to study my face in the rearview mirror. Juice stains, that's all. I flared my nostrils at my father's reflection to make him laugh, but he couldn't stop looking at Lila.

At the border they said we had to finish the cherries or throw them out. My father parked. We piled out and sat on the berm to eat.

I felt sick to my stomach when it was over. Pits, glistening with saliva and clinging fruit, freckled the asphalt. As we crossed the border an officer nodded as if we'd merely done our duty. Lila stuck her tongue out at him.

"Sit down and close your mouth," my mother said. My mother spoke rarely enough so that when she did, we listened. Still, my father's eyes flicked between Lila and the road all the way home.

After that, my father took Lila on special outings—breakfasts, bowling, movies with names that sounded R-rated. He and my mother sat me down to tell me Lila was having trouble in high school. She wanted to be too thin. She needed special attention.

They were so proud of me, my mother said. She put her hand on my father's knee. The air crackled, and he jerked away. "Static," he said, rubbing his thigh. My mother flexed her fingers.

The next summer, my parents took us to the islands for vacation. The humid air seemed to dampen whatever passed among us. We retold the story of our last trip so often that when someone said "cherries," we'd all start giggling. I said I'd always hoped that officer had planted them on the safe side of the border. My parents kept laughing, but Lila looked thoughtful.

My father sat next to me at a luau that night. He quizzed me on spelling words and cheered for each right answer—even *psoriasis*, with its surprising p and many s's. Then dancers came by to teach people the hula. My father waved me out of my chair.

On stage I wiggled my hips when I was told. Torchlight and applause made my cheeks flush with happiness. My family watched me from below. Lila was even eating, skewer after skewer of meats and pineapples.

She was still licking juices from the webs between her fingers when I returned. My father stared at me. The flush in my cheeks turned hard and frightening. I wanted to reverse myself, to walk backward onto the stage, un-swing my hips, sit down again and have no one notice me.

After midnight I woke to my father standing at the side of the pullout bed I shared with Lila. She was asleep; her deep breathing rattled the ancient bedsprings. Instead of sitting up, I reached my foot out as slowly as I could to touch Lila. The bedsprings paused. Then Lila stretched an arm overhead and reached toward my father. I closed my eyes, not sure why I felt relieved, and didn't open them again until morning.

Lila wasn't there. A pineapple sat on her pillow. Its spikes sliced my fingertips as I carried it into the kitchen.

When Lila didn't return by nightfall, my father called the police. My mother held the pineapple in her hands and hummed. The day before we left I sliced the top off the pineapple and planted it in the hotel's garden strip.

A month later my mother grilled an enormous fish for my father. The next morning he was dead. At his funeral, I caught a scaly sheen under his skin when I glanced away from his body. The doctor said a heart attack felled my father while my parents were having sex. Neither explanation is one I want to think about.

Now my mother mails ads to far-off newspapers with my father's photograph and the date of his death, in case Lila might see. When she thinks I'm asleep, she cradles me in her arms and whispers that even if I become beautiful, she'll never let anyone hurt me.

Her breath feels gentle as island air, warm enough so the boundary between skin and sky disappears. I want to tell my sister that it's safe now to push out roots, to grow.

THE COAT

THE COAT HAD TWELVE inside pockets: six on one side, six on the other. There were two pockets on the outside, too. On cold mornings, Jackson put his hands in the outside pockets as he sat behind the card table that he covered with a bright piece of fabric. But the inside ones were what always interested the police, the ham-handed muggers, and even a few of his customers, who would look over his spread of belt buckles from New Mexico and earrings from South America and bracelets from Thailand and then peer at his overstuffed coat for the real treasures that he kept close to his chest.

When the police and the muggers looked inside, this is what they found: not much. A pink dumbbell from a fitness club. A flashlight. A handful of lead washers. A feather. The police, in particular, would laugh when they'd do periodic shakedowns at the park where he slept sometimes, pulling out each item and holding it up to anyone who might be watching. Jackson knew they needed to look like they were doing something when they couldn't find any drugs.

Sometimes the police replaced everything back where it belonged. Sometimes they didn't. The muggers never laughed. They didn't take anything out, either, once they saw that the inside pockets were full of junk. They'd just kick him in the stomach, but at least then he wouldn't have to reorganize the coat. Jackson needed to know exactly what was in each pocket so that he could adjust his altitude quickly, without thinking about which pocket to reach into to rebalance his weight. Because that was the treasure he held closest to his chest, the one that no one could see. With the coat, he could fly.

He'd first seen the coat as he walked to class five years earlier, the day after a big windstorm. At first he'd thought the dingy coat was a plastic bag caught up in the tree. Then he'd seen a dangling sleeve.

The coat stayed in his mind all day. On his way home, he climbed up into the tree and tried to untangle it. As he unhooked a button from a twig, it felt as if a gust of wind blew through him and hit the coat, which almost sailed out of his hands. He grabbed it, stuffed it inside his shirt, and climbed down. As he walked to his apartment, he felt suddenly happy. He thought he was happy because of the lightness in his chest, but later he realized it was the coat trying to take flight.

He thought about calling his parents, who lived in the small town that Jackson had been straining to leave ever since he had seen a map. They didn't really understand why he wanted to go to college, or what he did there; when they did talk, he told them he was becoming a doctor, because his parents watched a TV show about a hospital and he thought it was something they would understand. Instead, he took language classes and sat in the library basement with enormous headphones muffling his ears, listening to recordings of people speaking Spanish and Portuguese and French and Mandarin. The sound of the voices felt at first like water gushing from a faucet. He loved the sensation of understanding that came when words began to distinguish themselves into individual droplets.

As he climbed the apartment stairs with the coat crushed against his ribs, he realized his parents would think it was strange if he called them just to tell them a story about a coat. In the end, he decided against calling them at all. Even though they all spoke the same language, they never could understand each other.

Jackson took the coat down to the basement to run it through the washing machine. He put it on as soon as it came out of the dryer. Maybe he was lucky he was inside a building that first time, and maybe not. The coat shot up to the ceiling with him inside. Jackon's head smacked against an air duct. When he came to, he was on the cold basement floor with the coat pinned beneath him. His dead weight must have startled the coat enough to make it fall.

The next day, Jackson bought a motorcycle helmet. Late that night, he snuck the coat and the helmet into the university gym. The sound of his helmet connecting with the rafters sent a sick thwack echoing around the empty bleachers. To Jackson, it sounded like applause.

After that, he spent weeks tinkering with the right kind of ballast, what to carry in which pocket, how to navigate around rafters. Later, he would use what he carried in his pockets to steer him away from power lines and low-flying aircraft—the coat was that fast. He experimented with how to use the zipper that ran up the front of the coat. Pulling it up slowly, tooth by metallic tooth, seemed to settle the coat down when it was time to come to land again. Dirt and weather weighed the coat down, too; if he wanted to descend quickly, he looked for a smokestack or an oncoming squall.

The coat liked to travel. It seemed to prefer full moons, when the world below was bathed in silver. Jackson and the coat would cruise just at the cloud line, where the air was thin enough to make him feel pleasantly dizzy. Jackson wanted an excuse for all their travels, so he started buying jewelry because he could pack a few weeks' worth of inventory in a single bag, and the weight was not too difficult to account for when rebalancing the coat. He set up a table on Telegraph Avenue and sold to the students who walked by. He was traveling too much now to be one of them, and he had no use for language tapes when he could fly to hear the same words spoken on a sun-faded street.

Jackson gave up the lease on his apartment. He didn't need it—he had his coat, which, when he settled inside it under a tree, cinched itself around him like a sleeping bag. Jackson stored his table in the truck of another vendor who had become his friend, and as soon as his inventory started to run low, he and the coat would set off again in the night.

Soon, he wore the coat all the time. He was always worried that if he set it down by itself, he would have miscalibrated the weight and it would take off without him. In a pinch, Jackson could pin it under a rock or two if he needed to leave it for a moment. But something always felt wrong about this. Besides, people might ask questions. Why would you put rocks on top of a coat?

Every weekend he set up his table, laid out his wares, and hunched himself into the coat. The money people gave him slid into the right outside pocket. He made change from the left. At the end of the day, he folded up his table and took the money to the bank. Then he walked back to the park to sleep. Occasionally, when sales were slow, he would go to the phone booth outside of the university library and call his parents. They would listen to the stories he made up about people who came to the hospital where he told them he was a volunteer—all he had to do was look around him in the park at dawn to see the ailments that were waking their owners up to start another day on the street. His parents would ask him to call again when he could, in voices filled with a mix of pride and confusion, and, before signing off, they would say how much they would like to come visit if it wasn't so terribly, terribly far. Jackson would hang up the phone, knowing that if he left here by dinnertime, the coat would land him outside of his parents' home. They would just be turning on their prime-time shows.

Jackson had read once about an island in the South Pacific where, once a person left the village, he disappeared from the people's minds as well. When he returned, it was as if he had always been there. There were no welcomes, no farewells. Jackson understood this. Always, the people who he knew should have been most important to him had vanished for him once they were out of his sight. He came to understand that he needed to remember them in order to not hurt their feelings. In high school, he put an enormous photo of his then-girlfriend in his room, which had both pleased and embarrassed her. Now he kept a small photo of his parents in an inside pocket, along with a small calendar. Each month, he wrote a note to himself to call them. He never tried to explain this to his parents. "You don't have to make an appointment with me," his mother would have said. "Aren't I just sitting here in the house, like always?"

One autumn, everything quieted. Students passed him and kept their heads down. Day after day, he put the same wares out on the table and then loaded them back into his pockets in the evening. The coat felt heavy, sluggish. Jackson tried all of his friend's catch phrases—he even tried flirting with some of the young women who walked by, telling them how beautiful the gold would look against their skin, the gems no match for their eyes, until he realized that no one was interested in flirting with a man who wore a huge gray coat zipped up to the neck. Sometimes, late at night, he and the coat would hover around the school's bell tower, neither of them having much enthusiasm for anything more.

As the days shortened, a friend told him about a holiday fair at the museum downtown. "They're looking for just your kind of shit, man. Stuff that looks like it came right from a village in the Andes," his friend said. His friend sold glass bongs that he made in his garage and bumper stickers printed with band names and expletives. "But you'll need more of it—they want each person to have a full booth, not just a card table."

On the walk back to the park, Jackson's feet seemed to bounce off the pavement, and he hadn't even taken the pink dumbbell out of his coat. That night he borrowed a camping backpack from his friend. He hiked up into the hills until he found a clearing and unzipped the coat halfway. Jackson took the dumbbell, a brick, and an old-fashioned iron from the coat's inside pockets and put them in the backpack, which he held in front of him—the coat didn't seem to be affected by anything not contained within its own sleeves and lining. The coat hoisted him into the air and then beelined toward the south.

For a month, he visited the silversmiths of Mexico, jade carvers in Guatemala, jewelers in Rio selling tourmaline. The coat was willing to take him higher and faster than ever before, not seeming to notice that they carried more weight in the backpack than they had on past trips. Midair, they drew up next to geese heading south, paused as if at a stoplight, and then accelerated into the dark sky above. Jackson could almost hear the coat rev its invisible engine and laugh. He began packing boxes of things too large to fit into the backpack—woven blankets, pottery—and shipped them to the post office at home, addressed to himself.

Jackson and the coat landed in a beach town at the end of the month. Once the sun came up, Jackson and the coat spent the day wandering along the beach, stopping to look at the trinkets the women and men were showing to the sunbathers. Jackson began to realize he had an eye for this, peering into one open suitcase and spotting the pure gold pendant among the brass. He wondered if he should tell the woman who held out the case to him, her head tiny under a white hat, and then he also wondered for how little he could get it from her.

There was a shout from the water. When Jackson turned, he saw a head in the midst of the waves, bobbing up and down, arms windmilling beside it. A group of boys and girls on the sand were screaming and waving back, shouting to anyone who would listen that their friend didn't know how to swim.

Before Jackson knew that his feet had started moving, he was in the water, thrashing his way out to the boy. He could feel the current catch him, as if he was in a slingshot snapping out to sea. He saw a hand stretch above the waves and he grabbed it and pulled the boy to him. Jackson kicked his legs but the two of them started slipping under the water. With one arm around the boy's chest, Jackson began pulling things out of the coat, letting them sink to the bottom of the ocean, and slowly, slowly, Jackson and the boy began to drift toward shore.

On the sand, the boy pulled away from him and began to vomit. The boys' friends surrounded the boy but did not touch him. People came to Jackson with towels, pulling on his arms, clapping him around the shoulders, pressing drinks into his hand. The woman who had been offering him the trinkets came and sat next to him.

"I have told them it is not a good trick," she said. When Jackson turned to look at her, she smiled. "A tourist on the beach sees one of the boys in trouble. He panics, calls for help. The rest of the boys grab his things, and the drowning boy swims back in." She squinted out at the waves, where pelicans skimmed so low their gray wings nearly touch the water's surface. "This time, he went out so far he was really drowning. And you went right in, coat and all. There was nothing of you left behind."

Jackson looked down at his arms. They were bare, the dark hair wet and slicked down against his skin. "My coat," he said. "Where is it?"

The woman looked around. "I do not know," she said. "When you came out of the water, you were not wearing a coat. You were just carrying my grandson." At that moment, one of the boys came up to Jackson, looking sheepish.

"Did you see my coat?" he asked the boy. The boy shook his head.

The woman put her palm on Jackson's shoulder and heaved herself to standing. "We won't forget you," she said to Jackson.

"You can," Jackson said. "I'm not sure I want to be remembered."

She lifted a shoulder as if to say, what could she do about that? After a moment, he turned to tell her that she should sell the round gold pendant for much more than the rest, but the woman had already wandered away.

Jackson waited for three days for the coat to wash up on the beach. Then he called the bank where he had been putting the money from his coat pocket and bought a plane ticket home. Flying in daylight, looking through an oval window, he saw the colors of the fields as they rolled beneath him: pale yellow and brown, not the nighttime blues and grays he knew. A woman sat next to him—her jaw looked like a brick of gold, he thought, heavy and beautiful—and when the flight attendant came by, selling meals, the woman sitting next to him gave the flight attendant a ten dollar bill and handed Jackson a lunch. "You look like you lost your best friend," she said. "At least eat something." He did, gripping the backpack that he'd stuffed under the seat in front of him with his feet.

The next weekend people swarmed his booth at the museum, gasping over the bracelets he spread out on the blanket-covered tables, running their fingers through the fringes on the scarves. He had to borrow a cardboard box from someone at the museum to use as a place to put the money. He emerged from the museum blinking, having nothing but handfuls of bills and rolls of coins and no pockets in which to put them.

And then there was the woman from the plane, standing in front of him, holding her hand out. He put ten dollars' worth of quarters in her hand, the weight of which would have let him sink from a 10,000-foot ceiling to the top of the Golden Gate Bridge. He thought she would go away.

Instead, she rolled the sleeve of quarters in her palm for a moment and put it back in his hand. "I came to see you," she said. As he slipped the quarters back into his pocket, he was surprised: it felt as if he was lifting off again, even though the shabby soles of his shoes stayed on the ground.

Years later, she would tell their children how they met, sitting next to each other on an airplane. Her future husband had been looking out the window as the plane descended through clouds, the ground visible and then gone again.

He didn't remember everything, but he remembered this, too: The plane had caught a bit of turbulence and his stomach soared, and for a moment he thought he was in his coat again. Then he heard a hiss at his side. The woman next to him was squeezing her eyes shut, her hands grasping at the air. "I hate to fly," she said, her eyes still closed. "I just want to get down."

The only thing he had for ballast was his hand, and he slipped it into hers. "Hold this," he said.

SLOW MOTION

"YOU MADE ME LEAVE work for this?" Henry asked.

I could tell he was trying not to look at me by how hard he stared at the road, by how his hands gripped the steering wheel where they usually rested, tapping out a tune that I never knew. I pressed the handkerchief he'd given me against my nose.

"Charlie looks worse," I told him, even though I knew he'd seen Charlie. Henry and the principal had stood outside the school nurse's office, their arms crossed, and watched me and Charlie shake hands. I could still feel how easily my knuckles had fit into his left eye socket.

As soon as we'd opened our math books that morning, Charlie had started throwing pencils at my head. By lunchtime I couldn't take it anymore. When I got mad, things started moving really fast—elbows and fists and even teeth sometimes. This wasn't the first time it had happened.

"Why can't you be more like Bodie Bailey?" Henry said. "He wouldn't have let some jerk like Charlie get to him." Henry's face was long and sharp-looking, like a blade of grass that would not bend, no matter how hard the wind.

"He doesn't go to school," I mumbled into the blood that had dried around my mouth. Bodie Bailey. It was like a nursery rhyme.

Henry, that's my father, that's what he wanted me to call him. It was the first thing I remembered him telling me after my mother died. "We're a team, James," he said. "People on the same team call each other by their real names."

The only team I wanted to be on was the Giants. Barry Bonds was my favorite. My Uncle Jack, who lived in San Francisco, sent me newspaper articles about all the home runs Barry had hit. He told me Barry could read every single pitch like he was watching it move through Jello. By the time it got to the plate he knew exactly what to do.

I'd only seen a real baseball game once, when Henry had taken me to Uncle Jack's for the weekend a few years ago. Now Henry was always too busy. Baseball and produce had the same seasons.

The windows of the truck were closed, but I could feel heat pushing against the glass, even in April. Everywhere else, baseball season was just starting. We passed rows and rows of trees beginning to bud. I squinted down each row to see where it ended. The way they flickered by made it hard to know where I was.

When we pulled up to the Baileys' farm, Henry stepped hard on the emergency brake and yanked the door open. "You can either come help out or stay in the car," he said. I tugged the seat belt strap tighter across my chest. "Fine." He slammed the door and the truck shook.

He stormed off across the field, stomping between rows and rows of lettuce. I could see the Baileys—all five of them—rise up from where they crouched with bags slung over their shoulders. Mr. Bailey, his face pink under his big straw hat, Mrs. Bailey and the tent of her long hair, they moved together toward Henry, reaching out as he got closer.

Mr. Bailey slapped him on the back and Mrs. Bailey put her arm around Henry's shoulders. The school must have called here first;

he put the Baileys' number on any emergency forms because that's where he always was. They must have known more about me than I did myself.

Even Sage and Amber, almost as tall as their parents and glowing with tans I could see from here, reached out and patted Henry's arm. Bodie looked up at the truck, then back down at his work.

Bodie Bailey was my age, and until last year he'd been in school with me. He was a funny-looking kid, with shaggy hair sprouting down over his ears like fuzzy earmuffs, and he did everything right. He read thick books. He wore wool hats he knitted himself. And when he'd been in school, he'd always left class to take Spanish with the middle-school kids because he already knew everything.

Charlie used to pick on him. Bodie never said a word. He just took it.

I peeled the handkerchief away from my nose and touched my face. My nose had stopped bleeding. I tried a few sniffs: I could smell the sweat on Henry's handkerchief. I brought the handkerchief back up to my face. It held the sour-sweet smell of the back of his neck, which I only got to smell when he picked me up, and now that I was twelve that never happened.

When Henry came back, carrying a huge box on his shoulder, I stuffed the rag in my pocket. I didn't want him to see me sniffling into his handkerchief.

After we got home, he unpacked the vegetables and pulled out the newsletter that came with them. Each week, the Baileys' farm put together produce boxes for about fifty people who drove in from the city to pick up real farm food. The newsletter had recipes for the things the Baileys grew and a weekly update on the family. Henry saved each of these letters in a binder that he kept on top of the fridge. The newsletters were how I knew the Baileys were perfect.

Henry handed me the letter as he began to unpack. "Will you put this in with all the others?"

I took everything over to the table and flipped the binder open. Henry put the newsletters in clear plastic sheets so you could read the recipes as you made them but they wouldn't get messed up if you spilled something. I slid this week's newsletter in quickly, trying not to read it. Then I spotted Henry's name, so of course I did.

We want to thank a very important person at our farm: Henry Martin. Henry has been with us for nearly twelve years, and he keeps the farm running smoothly both when we're here and when we're away. When we headed to Tahoe for a much-needed break from the farm, Henry and his own little farm angel, James, kept the place going. You probably didn't even notice anything different when you picked up your boxes, except their bright, smiling faces instead of ours!

I rolled my eyes. During spring break Henry had taken me to the farm in the pouring rain. He handed me a bag so I could follow along behind him and collect cabbages. I tried to splash him as much as possible every time he bent over. Then he took me over to the compost pile. While Bodie Bailey was making snowballs—I read about it in the newsletter—I shoveled chicken crap and rotten vegetables.

All our children have exciting summers planned for themselves. Sage has an internship at our favorite local radio station, so tune in Saturday and Sunday mornings to 104.5 FM to hear his show. Amber works nearly full-time at the wildlife refuge—when she's not being her usual helpful self, spotting berries so ripe they won't make it to your house, but must be eaten right then! Last year, Bodie decided to finish up at Winters Elementary and begin home schooling. In his first year of self-directed education, he has already—

I snapped the binder closed.

In the kitchen, Henry hummed as he bent over the stove. "Did you see you made the newsletter?" he called to me over the vegetables sizzling in a pan.

At the beginning of June, the Baileys were going to the beach for the weekend, and Henry promised he would take me to a baseball game. "This is our last chance before the real harvest starts," he said.

I'd hardly slept the night before, I was so excited. If Henry asked, though, I was going to say the wind kept me up, the way it licked around the house all night.

We packed lunch the next morning for the ride. I couldn't totally escape the farm—our cooler was packed with Bailey fruits and vegetables——but at least it was going to be just the two of us. Well, us and Barry Bonds. And 30,000 fans. I couldn't wait.

The phone rang as Henry was putting everything in the truck. I answered.

"Hi, James, it's Jon Bailey. Is your dad around?"

Henry came up behind me and took the phone out of my hand. He stretched the cord until the coils straightened, then shut the door to his room behind him.

Five minutes later, he came out and set the phone back on the receiver. "Jon—Mr. Bailey—came back early because of the wind last night. All the nets came off of the berries." He paused. "Birds are going to get them, you know?" He held his work clothes in a pile under one arm.

I sat down on the couch and pulled at wisps of stuffing that had started to trickle out of one of the pillows.

"I'm sorry, James," he said.

He did look sorry, but I didn't care. I pulled out a chunk of stuffing as big as a melon.

"Will you stop that?"

I took out another. It was like cotton candy, which was something Henry wouldn't let me eat.

He set down his clothes on the table. Maybe he would stay. "I said, stop that."

I stopped. I threw it at him instead. The stuffing, although it had felt solid in my hand, stalled in midair and tumbled gently to the ground three feet in front of him. "You promised," I said. "Why is everything about the Baileys?"

He picked up the ball of stuffing, grabbed the pillow and stuffed it back inside. "I thought you'd understand," he said. "You know how the farm works. Things can't always be on the schedule I'd like them to."

"They're just strawberries."

"I know. They're just strawberries that make sure we can live in this house and have food to eat. Baseball doesn't do anything like that."

He paused. He was waiting for something, watching me. I kicked at the coffee table. Then he gathered up his things. "Maybe we can do it another time."

I shook my head. It wasn't even worth it any more.

After he left, I brought down the binder and flipped through it, trying to find clues as to what was so special about the Baileys. The binder had the family's story going back to before Bodie was born.

We're so thrilled, read one letter. *We're going to be having a new addition to our farm. Amber has started pulling together scraps for a baby quilt, and every morning, Sage presses his ear against my belly.*

Ugh.

Another letter: *Jon has been spending some time away from the farm recently. Hopefully you'll see all of us together again by September, when you come to the farm's fall picnic.*

Boring. I wanted to find out how the kids knew how to do all that stuff, why Henry wanted to spend all his time with them instead of with me.

I woke up later that afternoon with the binder still spread across my lap. I could feel a warm hand on my head, but when I opened my eyes, the feeling was gone. "Are you looking for a recipe?" Henry asked. He was leaning over the couch. The tips of his fingers were stained red with berries.

"Yeah," I said. "Only I can't find it." I could smell the sweet juice even as he moved away.

A week later, when school got out, Henry started taking me to the farm. He tried to tell me I'd have more fun there than at our house, with its small patch of grass in the backyard, surrounded by a sagging fence. I thought he really wanted me to learn how to be a Bailey.

He would wake me when it was still dark and drive us to the Baileys. Everyone else worked in the fields then, when the air was cool. I slept in the cab of the truck, and when it got too stuffy, I moved under a tree. Henry didn't make me do anything.

After lunch, everyone would rest until early evening. I took my lunch out beneath a tree and slept in the shade, or else wandered around the farm to whatever corner they weren't working on. I didn't want to be cooped up in the perfect house with those perfect people.

Then when the sun slipped down a little, the adults came back out, walked along the rows, stooped, and stood again.

That summer was so hot you could feel it starting to melt around you as soon as you woke up. The land was flat and stretched for miles. You could see the city of Sacramento and, on a very clear day, the Sierra in the distance. But there weren't many clear days. Like the heat, the smog settled over the valley and did not let up.

Early in the morning, every growing thing struggled to hold on to the last bit of moisture that came from some combination of dew and the elaborate watering system Mr. Bailey had installed. Tomatoes bulged off the vines; bright squash skins gleamed through the leaves like buried treasure. As the days dragged on, fruit trees began to sag with the weight they carried. It was beautiful, but I didn't want to tell Henry I thought so.

By afternoon, everything had lost its glimmer. The light was dry and made my eyes hurt, and the bright colors made the plants look overdressed.

Then in the middle of July we had a heat wave. "Do you want to come into the house today?" Mrs. Bailey asked me one morning when we pulled up. She reached out a hand as if to pat me on the head, but then changed her mind.

I said no. The sun had only just come up and already I was so hot I couldn't even sweat anymore, but I didn't want to go inside. I started walking across the farm to the best shady spot I'd found, in between two rows of corn. The next thing I remembered, Henry was carrying me inside his skinny arms. "You're staying here until it cools off a bit," he said.

Mrs. Bailey made me a glass of lemonade. "Make yourself at home," she said. "And when we take a break, you and Bodie can play. Won't that be nice?"

I nodded and tried to smile so she would leave me alone. I heard the screen door bounce behind her, then the shushing sound of Mrs. Bailey putting her outside shoes back on.

I waited until she had crunched across the gravel driveway and out to the fields. I waited even longer than I needed to, in case she came back to get something: a hat, some water, a bandana to tie back her thick, brown hair. My mother's hair had been the color of grass in summer, when it was golden on the hills. The last time I saw her, when I was six and she was in the hospital, she had only a few clumps left. I had cried and Henry started taking me outside—until I could calm down, he said. But she called me back to her and held my hand against her bald head, which felt spongy and cool.

I was going to figure out what was so great about the Baileys, and I didn't want anyone to stop me. I went through the kitchen and the dining room; while everything was bigger than in our house, nothing looked that different. I even pulled open the refrigerator, but they had all the same things we did.

I ate a handful of cookies I found in a blue handmade jar, then wandered back through the house. I explored the two downstairs bedrooms, which I figured from the pictures on the walls were Sage's and Amber's. The only interesting thing I found was a diary hidden at the back of Amber's sock drawer, but I couldn't get the lock open.

Bodie's room must be upstairs, I thought, right near his parents. That baby.

Rows and rows of pictures loomed at me in the stairwell. It was like the one fancy restaurant in town, where the front hallway was lined with pictures of all the famous people who'd come and eaten there. Charlie's parents owned the restaurant and he would always brag about who he'd met. He'd shaken hands with the governor, he said, right in the middle of dinner.

But these photos were all the Baileys. The Baileys skiing, the Baileys holding up pumpkins, the Baileys crowded around their dinner table. There were pictures of each of the kids by themselves: Sage with huge earphones cradling his head, talking into a microphone; Amber, her hair blowing behind her, holding a hawk on her gloved wrist. Bodie sitting in a hammock, reading.

At the very top of the stairs another photo caught my eye because there were different people in it. It had been taken out behind the house, the sky streaked with pink in the background. As I looked closer, I saw my face, and Henry's.

That had been the worst day of all. It had been the farm's picnic last fall, when a bunch of people had come in from town to see the farm. The picnic had dragged on from noon into the early evening, when someone found a baseball bat at the back of an old shed.

The Baileys and a few of their summer helpers played against me and Henry and the town folks. It was going all right until Bodie got up to bat in the third inning.

He reached for the first two that came by and missed by a mile. Then Henry, our pitcher, lobbed a slow one across the plate that nearly hovered in the air in front of him. Bodie clamped his teeth down on his tongue and swung. I tried to stare down my father from where I stood between the wooden crates that marked second and third. Why'd you give it to him, I thought, when the ball zipped by me.

Bodie's ball disappeared into the tall grass, and someone called out that it was getting too hard to see anyway. Even though he was the losing pitcher, Henry threw Bodie up on his shoulders and ran the bases with him.

Mrs. Bailey had to find me and drag me into the picture. In the back row, the brown faces of the Baileys and Henry shone. I crouched alone in the front, my arms crossed over my knees.

I didn't hear Mr. Bailey until he was two steps below me. "Are you looking for something?" he asked.

I jumped. "The bathroom."

"Just head straight down the hall. I was just heading that way myself, but I can use the one in the bedroom." He winked at me. Then he saw the photo. "That was a great day, wasn't it?"

I nodded. I could feel sweat on my cheeks.

"You can look around, you know. We don't have anything to hide." He waited for a moment. I didn't know what to say, so I didn't say anything. Finally, he stumped past me and along the hall. I crept into the bathroom, wiping my sweaty face with my T-shirt. When I heard him go past again, I peered around the bathroom door. I was going to run right by the picture and back downstairs, but when I got closer I couldn't help myself.

There was Henry's arm wrapped around Bodie's neck, and me alone in the front. After the flash had gone off, I'd tried to sneak away into the dusk, but Henry caught me by the arm.

"I can't believe you were so rude to Mrs. Bailey," he'd said.

"It's not fair. Why'd you give him such an easy pitch?"

Even in the gray light I could tell he was looking at me as if I was stupid, his mouth partway open, his eyes narrow. "He needed it."

What about me? I wanted to yell, but I just jerked my arm away and ran.

I didn't realize my eyes were closed until I heard the glass shatter. I opened them in time to see the heel of my hand right in the middle of the frame, covering the faces in the photo, while small, clear shards poured from the painting like a waterfall. I yanked my arm back and the rest of the glass collapsed onto the stairs. I crouched down and started scooping up the pieces. When the floor looked clean, I carried the broken glass in my cupped hands to the bathroom and shook the glass into the trash.

Back in the hallway, the picture frame listed to one side. I straightened it out and considered: the photo seemed a little smaller now without the glass, but it was possible no one would notice the difference.

Footsteps scratched along the gravel somewhere just outside the house. I shot down the stairs and sped into the living room. As I flopped onto the couch, I started to feel a dull ache in my right hand. A piece of glass was caught in the line that ran from the base of my palm to near my thumb, a fortune-telling line, though I didn't know what it meant. I tried to scrape the shard away with my fingers, but it wouldn't come out.

As the door opened, I pulled a blanket off the arm of the couch and spread it over me, hiding my hand.

Mrs. Bailey asked me if I wanted to sit with them for lunch, and when I shook my head, she brought me a tray with a sandwich cut into two triangles and three small cookies. I ate them with my left hand. I might have that glass in there forever, but I wasn't going to ask for help. Maybe it would just come out by itself if I waited long enough.

After I finished, I raised my head and saw Mrs. Bailey standing with her hand on Bodie's shoulder, whispering something in his ear. She pushed him forward, then went back into the kitchen.

Bodie came by the couch and looked down at me. "You want to come read in my room?" he asked. The blanket was starting to scratch my legs, and I realized if I stayed underneath it for the rest of the day, Henry would get suspicious. I got up and followed Bodie up the stairs, hoping he wouldn't notice the broken picture.

Bodie's room had one long window that looked out on the west side of the house, the one place I hadn't really explored. I stuck my head out of the window, wondering if I could climb out and go back to my spot outside. The trees were thick, but I could still see an old washing machine and a small hammock. It looked like the one in the photo of Bodie and his book. But the roof dropped off too steeply for there to be a safe way down.

Bodie took a book from a shelf and tucked himself up on his bed. I walked along the bookshelves, pretending to look for something to read, although I knew I wouldn't find anything. Bodie didn't like the same things I did. My finger brushed along the spines of the books. My palm still ached but I tried to ignore it so that Bodie wouldn't see.

"I've got some comic books over there," Bodie said, pointing to a pile stacked beneath the window. "Why are you holding your hand like that?"

I tucked my hand, which was throbbing now, behind my back. "I know how to read."

"I know," he said. "They're good."

I waited until his hair dangled down over his book again before I walked over to the shelf and picked up a stack of comics. I wasn't going to read these. I didn't care if they were the best ones ever. I went along the tidy bookshelf and pulled some books partway out, put others back in upside down. I shuffled them around, mixed them up, even dog-eared a few pages. Then I heard Bodie snore.

Bodie had flopped back across his bed, his book spread open on his chest. His body was completely still.

I tiptoed toward him. His mouth was open. He took small gulping breaths in his sleep. Bodie's face looked so smooth; his cheeks had a little blanket of fuzzy hair. He almost smiled in his sleep. His arms splayed out, the soft side facing up. They'd be so easy to pin down with my knees. He could have two black eyes before he even woke up.

Then I heard a funny laugh. I knew for sure it was Henry, but he hadn't laughed like this in ages—the sound was loud and light, the way I remembered him from before. I went to the window and heard Bodie gasp and sit up behind me. I couldn't see anything at first. I leaned farther out the window, hooking my stomach on the ledge so I wouldn't slip out.

I felt Bodie's hand on my back and thought he was going to push me. Instead he grabbed the belt loops of my shorts. "I got you," he said. "It's okay."

I wasn't sure about that. If it was me, I would have dumped him out the window right then. But his grip on me felt strong, and I couldn't help wanting to see what was happening outside.

Now I could see Henry and Mr. Bailey standing next to the hammock, underneath a tree. Mr. Bailey looked like he was telling a story, and I could see Henry's shoulders shake. They both seemed small from up so high; I was almost looking right down on the tops of their heads, at their hair matted down from their sun hats and sweat.

Mr. Bailey reached toward Henry and pushed back a hair from his forehead. Henry grabbed his hand and moved it to his mouth. Their heads started pulling toward each other like magnets.

I didn't see what happened next because Bodie yanked back on to drag me out of the window. I stood up and started to ask him what he'd done that for, when I saw that he was crying. And I couldn't figure out why, but I felt like crying, too.

"You baby," I said to him. "What's wrong with you?" My heart fluttered in my chest, it wouldn't slow down.

"It's been like this all year and you haven't even known." Tears dripped from his chin onto his shirt.

I wasn't going to cry. "What are you talking about?"

"I have to see them all the time. And you get to be at school all day." He glared at me, narrowing his eyes. "It doesn't even bother you. And it's all Henry's fault."

"Don't you talk about my dad." My hands were already around Bodie's neck, my thumbs pressing at the shallow diamond of skin at the front of his throat. I could feel his heart beating against my hands. I tried to look over his head but I couldn't help looking at his face. He looked just like I felt, scared and sad and angry all at once.

I dropped my hands and tried to shrug, like he wasn't worth the trouble. I felt so tired. The ache in my right hand was even worse; I cupped my other hand around it and held it against myself.

There was more laughter from outside, then more silence. Bodie went over to the window and shoved his arms against the sill like he was trying to stop himself from jumping.

"Can you see them?" I asked.

He shook his head. Then he started to yell.

"James is hitting me! Help!" I'd never heard him yell like that. He kept going until we heard two sets of heavy footsteps coming up the stairs. When we heard them Bodie sat back down on the bed, picked up his book, and started to read. I didn't know what to do so I grabbed a book too and went to the opposite corner.

Henry and Mr. Bailey pushed through the door, both out of breath. Henry looked ready to hit me himself.

Mr. Bailey said, "Well, it looks like the boys solved their own problem. See, you don't need to yell for me, Bodie. You can work it out yourself." He smiled and backed out of the room.

"Sorry, Dad," Bodie said.

Henry glanced from Bodie to me and back again. Bodie didn't have a mark on him except the streaks of dirt on his face. Henry stood there for a moment in the doorway, watching us. When Mr. Bailey's footsteps had faded from the stairs he turned and left.

That night, Henry told me I could stay home from now on. He left early in the morning, and I got to sleep in. I woke up sweating, with the sheets twisted up around my neck. My hand felt like it was on fire.

The house seemed quiet, even though it was small and every noise from outside leaked through the thin walls. I went into the bathroom and found bandages in the medicine cabinet and some of that cream that Henry put on cuts. I took it all to the kitchen table. I smeared the cream on top of the cut and added some extra to be safe. Then I made an X with the bandages to keep it all from leaking out.

From where I sat, I could see Henry's closed bedroom door. The two big knots in the wood glared at me like eyes.

We'd moved here after my mother died. Our other house was small, too, but it didn't feel like there were so many secrets. Now, he was always up before I was. The door stayed closed while he worked in the kitchen, and I never saw him go to bed. Even though Henry had never said anything to me, I knew I wasn't supposed to go into his room. I put the bandage wrappers in the trash and went to put my hand on the doorknob. I only meant to open it, to swing the door back so that it wouldn't watch me anymore. But once the door was open, my feet took me inside before I could stop them.

His bed was untucked, which surprised me because he'd taught me how to make my bed so it was crisp and felt good when you got in. Henry usually left the windows and doors open overnight, then closed them before we left the house to keep it cool. The curtains in front of the small window lifted slightly with the breeze. I went to the window and shut it, letting the heavy curtains sag back into place.

Inside his closet, clothes hung on a low wooden dowel, mostly work shirts and T-shirts, with one nice white one that looked stiff at the end. One tie was slung around a hanger. I'd only seen him wear it to the funeral. I pushed my hands through the clothes to see if there was something else hidden behind them. I wasn't sure what I was looking for.

There was a rustle outside. I yanked my hands back and ran to the doorway. The rustle went quiet. I waited for a few minutes for my heart to stop pounding before I went back in.

There wasn't much else in the room, just a small nightstand next to the bed, with a square drawer that was stuck halfway open. Inside were some bills, a postcard from my uncle—he'd gone on a trip somewhere—and one from the Baileys on their trip to Tahoe, addressed to both of us. There were some crumpled-up receipts. I took them out with my fingertips—the cream was starting to leak out of the bandages—and spread them against the bed. The one at the bottom was bigger than the others, already smoothed out and blank on one side. I turned it over.

It wasn't a receipt at all. It was a drawing I had done a few years before. I'd made it with the new crayons I'd gotten, first day back to school, when Bodie was still there too. There was a lollipop figure with a triangle for a red cape, and I'd scrawled "Dad" across the top. I'd been proud of it right when I'd finished it, the crayon dark and sharp, I felt sure of myself. Then I'd seen Bodie's drawing. The teacher held it up for us. It was of his family, the five of them, and I saw that their eyes looked like real eyes, not black dots, and their feet weren't duck-footed like the ones I'd drawn. I'd crumpled up my drawing and stuck it in my backpack. But here it was again, only a ghost of wrinkles beneath the bright superhero who once was my dad.

When he came home Henry asked if I wanted to go into town and run errands with him. I didn't really want to, but something about seeing that drawing again gave me a little surge of goodness, so I agreed. I wanted him to tell me something, anything, to put things back in the order I knew they belonged in. On the drive he kept watching me from the corner of his eye, his mouth starting to open, but when we got into town, he dropped me off at the park and said he'd be back in ten minutes, he had to do something at the bank.

I found the small playground and sat in one of the swings. I held onto the chain of the swing with one hand and let the bandaged one rest on my knee. Trees grew on all sides of the playground, and the wind had started to slap against their leaves. The sky above me turned gray, then darkened. Maybe the heat wave was going to be over. Maybe we'd get some rain.

Someone pushed me from behind, and I hit the ground hard. I turned to look behind me and I saw the swing coming at my head. I reached up and grabbed it, then used the seat of the swing to pull myself up.

Charlie stood on the other side of the swing. He didn't say anything; he just cocked his arm back and then I saw his fist heading toward my face.

That's when I figured out I could make things happen in slow motion. Charlie's fingers squeezed together, his thumb shifted forward, then back, as if checking whether it was in the right position. His knuckles glided closer and closer to my face, and as I moved my head out of the way I saw my breath ripple the tiny hairs on his finger like a wave of wind through the Baileys' autumn corn. Behind this I saw his face, the freckles bunched up, his black hair plastered on his forehead from the heat. I moved my head away, and now his fist swung through where I had just been. The rest of his body followed, making him stumble and land on his knees.

He pushed himself up again and dove at me. The same thing happened: his arms reached out, his body eased forward through the air, and I stepped to the side before everything sped up to normal, and he sailed forward and thudded on the sand. The swing hung there between us, the chains creaked as they swayed back and forth in the growing breeze.

He lifted his head from the ground. I could see his mouth start to open, and I slowed it down, too. His mouth looked like it was chewing something sticky, wrapping around the words as they came out. "You fag," Charlie said, finally. "You and Bodie Bailey."

I took a quick breath in. I had never been sure what the word meant. Charlie's eyes went big, as if he wasn't sure either. We both knew whatever he said meant too much to just hit back. If I did something, I would have to kill Charlie, and I couldn't, even though he was starting to look like he wasn't surprised anymore. "It's not true," I said, instead.

A small mean smile was starting up on his face. It was slow enough, though—I made everything slow enough—so that as I walked away, I could imagine that what he said still somehow hadn't reached me yet.

Henry picked me up at the curb. The truck started vibrating as it sped up, the air thumping through the windows. We sailed down the main road, and I saw thick clouds coming in from the west. I stuck my hand out the window and felt the wind pushing against it. Suddenly my hand stung and I yanked my hand back in.

"Are you all right?" Henry asked. He pulled the truck to the patch of dry grass on the side of the road. He grabbed for my hand. When he saw it, he blew through his teeth. He tilted his head and squinted at me like he was going to ask me something, but instead he reached into his pocket for his jackknife.

"Never thought I'd really use these," he said, working out the tweezers hidden inside the knife. Henry bent down over my hand, and I felt a sharp pinch. I didn't say anything. After a minute, he held the tweezers up. "I think I got it," he said. "Do you want to take a look?" I shook my head.

He tossed the piece of glass out the window. We sat there for a while, him watching me, me looking down at my hand. I could feel the truck's dark rattle as other cars sped past us. "Do you want to talk?"

"No," I said. "No." My hand was cooling down. I looked up at him. "It's okay."

He nodded once, turned the key and pulled back onto the road.

That night, lightning flashed all around our house, and I sat up in my bed, my hands wrapped around my knees, and wondered if Henry was doing the same thing in his room, sitting and looking out the window. It was just heat lightning, though. It never rained that night.

My dad and Uncle Jack are passing a beer back and forth over my head, and I keep trying to grab it to make them laugh. It's the last home game in September, and we sit just to the left of the batter's box, almost straight behind home plate. I can see Barry when he comes up to bat. We're so close I can even see the black number 25 on his shirt move up and down as he breathes. The pitcher winds up, and I squint to watch the ball like Barry watches it, slowing the ball down, making sure it's in just the right place.

He hits two home runs, one in the third, one in the sixth, not enough to save the game. I know he is going to do it each time, I am seeing exactly the same thing, all in slow motion, and I would swing if I had a bat in my hands.

During the seventh-inning stretch, we all stand up and shake out our arms and legs and sing "Take Me Out to the Ballgame." When we sit down again, my dad hands the beer to me. "Here, have a sip," he says.

I taste it and it's bitter, but I smile all the same.

My dad seems not to notice that I've stopped calling him Henry. Somehow when you've seen something you shouldn't, it's harder to be friends.

Barry doesn't get up again, so I start watching the umpire, the beer still making my tongue ache. I suddenly want to be the umpire more than anything, wishing I could do what he does when someone calls time. He holds up his hands and everyone backs away, gets settled, nudges the dirt off their shoes.

Then the umpire pulls his mask down, squats behind the catcher. The ball comes in from the pitcher's mound. But instead of a ball I see my dad's head leaning toward Mr. Bailey's. It's getting closer and closer, and as soon as they touch, things will never be the same, and I'm not sure what I should do. After it happens, I will have my dad. But there will always be the moment right before when I will never be anything like Bodie Bailey. Hold on, I want to say, putting my palms up and out. Stop it. Stop it right there.

GOLDEN HOUR

AS SOPHIA PACKS TO LEAVE, Miles tells her that he's really almost done with the boat. Soon they will sail out of Monterey Bay and turn south to find the place they were meant to be. Sophia says that he is asking for more time than she can give, and that if he could see that he was already in the place he was meant to be, she wouldn't be leaving.

She tries to give him the watch back before she takes the train to her sister's farm in New Mexico. "No, you keep it," he says. "Sorry it can't give you back the time you wasted here."

In the days after she leaves, Miles texts Sophia the questions he meant to ask. *Won't you miss the water? Does everyone really wear cowboy boots and put green chile on everything? Have you seen any aliens yet?*

When she doesn't respond, Miles begins taking photos of the sunset for her. This is what had pulled them together at the end of each day, the golden hour before the sun fell beneath the horizon, the blue hour of twilight that followed.

Before she left, their mornings had a regular rhythm, too. Sophia would leave before dawn for an early shift at the café in Moss

Landing. Miles would work on the boat until she returned, and they would both work some more. Sophia pulled out her sewing machine, made sails and jacklines, fixed covers and canvas and upholstery. She sang to herself all the while. Bits of songs—she'd never been in one home long enough as a child to learn a whole lullaby. Miles loved the patchwork songs, and the boat seemed to respond, too, swaying beneath them as they worked, even when the harbor water beneath them was a still, sullen green.

In the late afternoon, Miles would ring the bell in the cockpit— eight rings, signaling the end of a watch. Then they would motor out as far into Monterey Bay as the boat could manage. He and Sophia would watch the sunset. They talked about how different the sun would look on the open ocean, when the ignorant fist that was the land didn't tug back at them anymore.

Miles doesn't ring the bell anymore. The boat is timid and touchy without Sophia; the bolts he has just replaced loosen and rust. Still, some of the sunsets over the bay are clear, the sun knocking cleanly against the rim of the horizon. Other times the sunsets are blood- red, striped with clouds, or too foggy to see. Occasionally Miles will send a note along with the photo: *No green flash yet!* Or *There's a fire somewhere that's making this beautiful.* Once, a sea otter bobs next to the boat and cracks open the sea urchin on its chest to the same rhythm that Miles types out his messages.

Sophia never replies. Six weeks later, Miles runs out of money and he gets a text back telling him that he has THE WRONG NUMBER AND DON'T YOU HAVE ANYTHING BETTER TO DO THAN WATCH THE SUN SET?!? Miles gets a job on a construction crew and sells the boat to a woman who plans to name it *Unsinkable II.* He and Sophia had been waiting for the boat to be done to agree on a name. "What happened to the first Unsinkable?" Miles wants to ask the woman, but the boat is already on the trailer and pulling away.

Miles hears a thin whimper. The boat? No, it's the harbormaster's dog, wheezing in its sleep. Or maybe he is hearing himself: Miles's chest feels like someone is pulling duct tape off the skin, piece by piece. He touches his back pocket, where he put the woman's check, until the feeling goes away.

Sophia loses her cellphone at Union Station in Los Angeles, but she can't seem to lose the watch. By the time the train arrives in Albuquerque, Sophia can't even rally enough energy to unbuckle the watch from her wrist, even though the dial that shows the time in Roman numerals is now always an hour behind. Miles gave it to Sophia when sailing to find a new home was something they had dreamed up together, rather than an idea he had put on her like a too-warm coat. "It came with the boat," he told her.

Maybe Sophia would like the watch if she understood all of its features. On the boat, she hadn't helped Miles with the more involved mechanical issues. Getting that deep into the boat's inner workings seemed like it would be trespassing—too close to Miles's heart or to the boat's, she wasn't sure.

A semicircle cutout on the watch face shows the phases of the moon. Another set of dials tracks sidereal time, measured by observing stars. "It's a little less than four minutes shorter than a regular day," he had explained.

At first, the spinning of the different dials—complications, Miles called them—fascinated Sophia. But soon the watch felt too much like the two of them, slightly off cycle, judging their position against different points in the sky.

Now Sophia turns the face of the watch toward the inside of her wrist so she won't snag it against anything at the new restaurant where she works, a place where each of the dishes has the name of some desirable quality—*Empathy Pancakes, Sweet Potato Devotion*. Outside the restaurant is a river filled with rocks and the pink fringes of thistles. Dust and altitude and parched air exhaust her. She sleeps readily, heavily.

One Monday she walks to the library after work to wait for her sister, Mia, who is out delivering farm boxes. Sophia sits with a book in one of the stuffed armchairs and closes her eyes. Only the pulsing suck and hum of the vacuum rouses her, hours later.

The man pushing the vacuum is wearing a striped button down and dark pants with pink socks that flash out from underneath the cuffs. He says something to her, and she shakes her head. He bends to click the vacuum off. "The children's area is closed," he repeats. "But the makerspace upstairs is still open."

The makerspace is a room enclosed in glass in the center of the library. The overhead lights inside are aggressive and there is a huddle of preteen boys in baseball caps and braces. There is also an empty chair. Sophia sits and puts her head down on the table.

"Here's what you need to get going," a voice says. It is one of the boys, this one with a worried smile. "We're making circuits." He gives names to the pile of supplies he pushes in front of her: copper tape, batteries, LED light. She wants to glare at him until he migrates back to his friends, but her traitorous fingers reach for the copper. Five minutes later, the small green light flashes on and off, on and off. Every time the light goes on a small hum of pride ignites in her throat. She returns, night after night, for this feeling.

The man who sits in the back booth at the restaurant a few weeks later reminds her of Miles, although she can't say why. This man has a scraggly ponytail and perfect white teeth, while rumple-haired Miles had two front teeth that overlapped slightly, as if embarrassed to show all of themselves. Sophia carries a cup of coffee toward the man's table, the saucer taut between her hands so that it doesn't spill. The bell on the front door rings. A woman wrapped in scarves—they cover her head, her shoulders, her waist, they drag from her like tails—has started through the door only to be caught halfway, several grocery bags in each of her bundled arms.

Sophia sets the coffee on the front counter and goes to the door, pulling at it with both hands. The wind outside yanks back.

Finally, the door gives. "Thanks," the woman huffs, and pushes past her. Sophia peers up at the mechanism that is supposed to prevent the door from slamming. She wiggles the door back and forth, and the bell rings over and over.

"What about my coffee?" the man calls from the back. "I see it sitting right there."

"One moment," Sophia says. She stares at the mechanism, trying to imagine how it works.

"Hello!" The man stands up and his chair shudders away from him. "Are you going to bring me my coffee or do I have to get it myself?"

Several things then happen at once. The man pushes through the tables and grabs for the coffee. The woman in the scarves swings one of her bags around as she takes a seat. Sophia senses exactly what is wrong with the mechanism. The spring inside the door closer is too tight. If she loosens the screws on the bottom, it can swing more freely.

Sophia turns to get the screwdriver from beneath the cash register and the man trips over the woman's bag and the coffee flips over in the air and onto the checkered linoleum floor. "Jesus," he says, pulling his stained shirt away from his body. "What is wrong with you people?"

The woman unwraps a purple scarf from her right arm and begins to dab at the man's shirt without speaking. The man arches away from her, disgust widening his face. "Get away from me," he says. He is nothing like Miles, Sophia realizes, and, for the first time, she misses Miles and his rumpled hair and relentless hope.

The cook, a narrow woman with a face ancient as sandstone, strides out from the kitchen with a whisk and levels it at the man. "You—out!" she says. To Sophia's surprise, the man scrambles over himself to get to the door, where he is caught for a moment, halfway out, before slipping away. "Some people," the cook says.

Her face erodes into a smile that scans over Sophia, taking in Sophia's tentative mirror of a smile, the screwdriver in the girl's hand, the way her apron hugs against her belly. The cook sighs, and Sophia has another sudden understanding about the strange exhaustion she's been feeling, about the way parts fit together to make something new.

Mia and her husband, George, have bees and chickens and goats and, now, Sophia. Their fingernails have half-moons of dirt and their backs ache and they have no money to fix the cracked window of their truck. They say they are happy to have Sophia. The jars of honey set on the kitchen counter glow like stained-glass windows, amber and yellow and brown. Sometimes Sophia cries when she sees the light pour through them.

Mia tells Sophia to take a pregnancy test to be sure. George says Sophia can use any tool he has as long as she puts it back where she finds it and doesn't hurt herself. The librarian in charge of the makerspace has seen how Sophia works with the tools, and he begins to show her how to disassemble a basic mechanical watch. After work, she studies the watch that Miles gave her. She draws pictures of the watch face and its visible complications—the moon that rises and sets, a dial that indicates the ups and downs of tides. Then she imagines how the inner layers of wheels and bearings fit together. She sketches their placement, tries to understand how the watch could come apart and come together again.

One night, Sophia removes the case back and peers into the inner workings. She uses a tiny screwdriver and tweezers to gently take apart the watch. There is only one piece she finds that is unknown to her, a small gear that is stamped with a pair of wings. She asks the librarian about it, and when he doesn't know, they pore over the library's small collection of watchmaking books.

In the end, she finds nothing. She cleans the winged gear, along with the rest of the mechanism, and begins to set each part gently back in place. Hundreds of miles to the west, the boat twitches on its tie-down. There are gulls overhead and the domino line of dock planks and to the west, the pull of the sea. Sophia works on into the night, and the fibers inside the distant knots ease their grip on each other, relax their vigilance. In the morning a piece of rope will be found on the dock, curled up onto itself like a baby.

Miles is driving up the coast after work when he feels something following alongside him. The muscles in his chest ache from levering lumber into place for the entryway of a house that will overlook the sea. He can't look away from the road, which is lined with crosses and plastic flowers to mark where someone watched the water a moment too long. The hovering presence stays just beyond his shoulder, like how the moon used to follow him from the window of his parents' car. His parents are long dead and so is the feeling of being taken somewhere that he knew was home.

The followed feeling doesn't lift—sometimes he imagines that it is a pelican, flying low over the water. Sometimes he imagines it is Sophia. One evening the setting sun bores into his eyes and he can't take it anymore. He pulls across the centerline to the guardrail and flings himself out of the truck. There is a flapping down below him. Miles scoops up a stone from the dazzle of broken glass and bottle caps on the shoulder and hurls it toward the sea. Floating there, far past the range of Miles' tired arm, is the boat. Miles waves, and the boat's sails raise themselves, as if it sees him, too. And then the entire boat hoists itself off the surface of the water and comes to meet him.

Sophia falls asleep in her clothes again at the workbench, her zipper pressing a jagged pink line of teeth into her belly. She has another vivid dream, in which the boat hangs over her like the moon and she gives Miles the watch back and tells him that he has given her another kind of time.

When she wakes, she yawns and stumbles outside into a spring night thick with honey and impatience. She brushes this away. She will make so many things in her own time, which now grows at a different pace than any complication. Sophia's time is now the size of a plum. In two weeks, it will be a pear. By the end of summer, time will swell to the size of a cherimoya, that sweet, strange fruit that her sister fed her the other day, its green outsides with round markings like petals, like small fingerprints.

ST. LUCIA BRINGS THE LIGHT

LUCY HAS HEARD there is a woman up in Boston who is in charge of cataloguing the stars. The woman makes lists of stars and puts them into categories. She has never married and the astronomers, all of them men, listen to her.

Lucy can hardly see the stars here in New Jersey but she would split them any which way if someone actually stopped to listen. Alphabetical, numerical, by color like how her mother puts the handkerchiefs in her father's dresser drawer. He's not a fancy man—he works at the brewery in Orange—his nose just always runs.

Hardly anybody listens to Lucy. "Why don't you like that Joe? He's got a good job." Says her mother. Says her older brother. Says her older sister: "You have to marry someone, Lucy."

I don't, she thinks. *I won't.*

Her friend Pihla is the one somebody who understands. The winter they are both thirteen, Pihla sneaks Lucy into the the Lutheran church to watch as a young girl is crowned with a wreath of candles. "*You* should be Saint Lucia." Pihla grins at Lucy, her white teeth gleaming in the flickering light.

Lucy kisses her friend's round cheek. She does not need to tell Pihla that this is exactly what she wants, to feel like she is made of light. The two of them spend as much time as they can parading around town with their arms linked, or talking about being Anne Bonny, the lady pirate, sailing the warm seas of the Caribbean, or Annie Oakley, wielding her gun. Lucy dreams, too, of being the girl with flames around her head who delivers saffron buns. The two girls spend as much time together as they can, because soon they will be married, apart, and like their mothers, have little time to dream.

Then, the war! The older brothers and handsome Joe leave and the mothers leave the girls be as they focus on their own private worries. Lucy and Pihla at 16, at 17, at 18–still together, still dreaming, longer than they ever expected. Then the dream unfurls new wonders: they are offered jobs at the dial factory, where they can sit next to each other all day painting marks on clock faces so that the soldiers can tell time in the dark.

They make time now. Lick the end of the brush, dip it in the paint, dot the end of the brush against the clock. Undark, the paint is called, made with the brilliance of radium. At night, it glows on Lucy's apron. At night, she glows. This is far better than being able to put the stars in order. If your own skin is radiant, who cares who is listening?

She and Pihla are giddy, luminous. Not just their skin. Their lives. They come home with money in their pockets. Some weekends they go all the way to the beaches on Staten Island and dip in the cold water, come out shivering and free. They don't need to pretend they are pirates any more. They have already stolen away with the treasure they always wanted: themselves.

Then the bright hands shift. The girls' teeth loosen in their jaws. At first when the doctors come, they call it syphilis, or poor breeding. Pihla has always been stronger, her name means rowan tree, but she goes first: her gums become checkerboards, one piece taken, then another. More doctors come, their coats white as her sweet friend's teeth once were.

Now they come to Lucy, too. Doctors first, then the men in suits with their glasses and their furrowed brows, the scratch of their pens against paper that means money, someday. For someone else: she will not live to see it. Still, will they believe her if she says it was the best job in the world?

Soon, she will no longer be able to raise her hand to take the oath when the judge asks if she will tell the truth. For now, the men sit by her side, attentive. It is the glow around her, she knows it: she doesn't need to be an astronomer, her own body is the star. She will tell them again and, at last, maybe they will listen.

HOW TO CAPTURE CARBON

PARENTS START PREPARING their children for middle school early now. Even before they are old enough to read, there are tutors, educational videos, flashcards. The flashcards have diagrams or letters or pictures, or sometimes all of these things, depending on the target age.

The flashcards for the youngest children start with the basics. O is for Oxygen. But how do you explain something so invisible, necessary, fragile? To help, many of the flashcard sets come with sample scripts for parents who are too old to have gone to middle school and learn the things that middle school children do now.

For oxygen, the script suggests: *Oxygen is even better when it comes in pairs. Here is a picture of a tree exhaling. A tree, yes, that's what that is—you may not have seen one before.*

For carbon: *Here it is, the letter C. It is pencil scrawl and diamond and star spew. Look, there are its four welcoming arms.*

Now this one, the parents might say. This one has both carbon and oxygen. See? Carbon dioxide. You are right, the carbon's two pairs of arms are reaching out on either side. It comes between the oxygens and they can no longer be dance partners. You are right, the carbon looks kind of like half a spider. No, my love, we don't smash spiders. But we would smash this carbon dioxide if we could. We want it to become something else. That's what trees did, they got the pair of oxygens away from carbon and put them back together again. Now, instead of trees, we have middle school.

People gave me flashcards soon after my first daughter was born, and neighbors pressed them into my full hands when I was pregnant with my second. I never showed my daughters the flashcards. I felt foolish talking about something I didn't really understand, ashamed that I didn't understand it. Instead, we played capture-the-flag in the winter when the air was clearer, my girls' wild feet running over the bare dirt. Sometimes in the summer, too, if we woke early before the smoke had settled too close to the ground. If we were lucky, there would be a breeze, and the air would feel like the past, like pleasure.

Even without the flashcards, my girls were enough: now they, too, wear the green uniforms and the neighbors' faces are photovoltaic with pride as we walk by on the way to the schools. None of us have seen the inside of the school, but we can imagine it: these brilliant minds bent over laboratory benches, finding new ways to capture carbon. We have visions of equations, protective goggles, Nobel Prizes. My girls' uniforms have badges with a pair of oxygens, holding hands. Twin molecules.

My girls are not twins. I have two girls, because they say two is the right number. Somehow there are not supposed to be more people, because more people make more carbon dioxide, but they also say we need enough people so that we can all take care of each other. They say the math works out.

My older girl is Nest. A name with utility. A name of something once found in a tree. We must be useful now, thoughtful, hopeful, selfless. All the things we were not during my own childhood, which at the time seemed simple but now people think of as reckless and ignorant.

When I was pregnant with Nest, I read all about pregnancy and birth and babies so that I would be ready. They say the act of making flashcards is what helps you remember things, so I wrote out by hand each concept I didn't know. Gravidity, BPAs, Cluster Feeding, SIDS. I followed the waterfall method, placing the flashcards that I knew in one stack, and working with smaller and smaller stacks of unfamiliar words until I could remember them all.

When Nest was born, her eyes were so wise it was as if she held me, as if I were the egg. I didn't need to look at my flashcards anymore, with my reflection now nestled within her pupils.

The year she was born was when they started talking about the capturing in earnest, how it would solve everything, how the children would lead us. As Nest got older, she and I built card houses out of all of the flashcards, leaning Sulfur Dioxide up against Multiparous. Sometimes Nest's father helped. He is a big man who does what he is told.

Maybe, when I wasn't looking, he showed her the flashcards as we were all instructed. Maybe that is how she got into middle school. They only take the best of the children, and she did not get the best from me. As a child, I was always looking out the window at the sky, not knowing that I should remember how blue it was.

My younger girl is Pearl. A pearl is something captured inside an oyster. Made after years of wearing down and wearing away. Birth is sometimes called confinement, but it could be called containment, captivity. You are forced inside yourself to bring something new out, and you are never really free again. I didn't want to be free, not from my daughters.

Now, as we walk to school in the smoke-light, Pearl's skin looks orange and iridescent. Looking at her, at both of them, I am an empty oyster. Proud, but lonely, too. We walk together, one of them on each side. If I had four arms to hold them, I would. Instead, I drop them off at the gate, and they go in to do the good work, capturing the carbon, and I go home and stay inside until it is time to pick them up.

At home I have trouble keeping the curtains closed, even though it keeps our house cooler and blocks out the strange skies. Through the windows, I can see the stumps that my friends and I once used as bases for our games, the place where we would draw a line in the dirt to separate the sides. There had been many children in the neighborhood then. If enough of us got captured by the other team, we would link arms to make a chain leading out from the jail—an old patch of deer brush—so that someone from our team could rescue us. Sometimes, we all forgot about the flag because it was so much fun to run and tag and get free.

Now there are so many things we can't forget. There are no more outside games. Those of us who are not doing the capturing must keep ourselves inside, away from the bad air. If we get sick we will make more work for everyone.

At the end of the day, I layer myself in protective clothes and face scarves, grays and yellows and browns, and walk back to school. The girls come out glassy-eyed and quiet. It is a long day at school, but they say it is necessary for them to learn everything they must do.

When they first started, the girls would come home ravenous. They craved tri-tip and mashed potatoes with pools of gravy. The school sent messages home to the parents: we were to ignore their hunger—they were being fed a balanced diet in class to support their learning. *There's an adjustment period*, the parents would say to each other at the gate. *Don't you remember middle school? I'd never go back.*

I tried to do what they said. But late at night, when the girls would wake half-dreaming, sometimes I would make them spaghetti with butter and cheese. They slept more soundly, looked more like themselves, like children, instead of undersized adults with faces shut like all the doors.

Now the parents don't talk at the gates any more. Our own adjustment period has passed. When my girls were little, their toes were so strong that they could cling to my hair with their feet and hang upside down like bats. We would walk like that as the sun rose, their warm bodies wind-chiming gently against my back. Now I want to be the bat, swooping them up under my leathery wings.

The parents have been told not to ask them too much about their day; it may be some time before they can explain what they are doing in a way an older, guiltier generation can understand. Instead we walk home, like bats only in that we are silent, silent but for a few small clicks of our tongues.

In the mornings I try to watch through the gates. I look for flags. I look for children running, but the air is too thick with the elements I can't remember, and I am too ashamed about my own childhood. How happy it was, how little I thought about the future.

Instead, I ask one of the recommended questions. "Do you love it?"

"Yes," they say. "We love it."

I start asking them every day.

Before they were born, I took in ironing and mending. There has been less and less work over the years, because now we are to focus on the world around us, not the small details of the inside of our homes. Still, I iron while they are gone. I iron napkins and pillowcases. I iron bedsheets and towels. I take the curtains down, one at a time, and iron them, too, even though the closed windows will never let in a breeze to blow and wrinkle the fabric.

I capture the water from the laundry and use it in the toilet. I capture the water from the shower and use it in the sink. I recycle the air, I reuse the bottles, I make dinner out of leftovers, and then make breakfast out of dinner. My house is a container, everything trapped inside. I imagine the girls at school, learning how to do the same thing, to capture, and I feel calmer.

One day, on the way home from school, Pearl burps. It is long and loud and exuberant and I remember that she hasn't been any of those things in weeks. "Oh, Pearl," I say, trying not to smile. "Is some boy in your class teaching you how to burp the alphabet?"

The girls look at each other. "There are no boys," Nest says.

"Boys are not allowed to do what we do," Pearl says.

"What do the boys do?" I ask. They look at each other again and say nothing. For a moment, I feel relieved for the girls. They will not have to become oysters. They will not one day be emptied of their great treasure; it will always be their own. Yet after they go to bed and my husband is reading the news again, even though it only makes him sad, I make a list called "All the boys I've loved but not like that."

At first, I write names, but then this seems embarrassing, and I just put initials. In case my husband finds us. By us, I mean me and my list, because he will not be jealous of the boys, but he will be jealous of the list. Because I am so good at capturing these things and writing them down, while he can only go to work and come home again and read the news and feel sad. No wonder the boys are not doing the good work my daughters do.

Late at night, they come downstairs in their nightgowns and ask for spaghetti. "They dissemble things," Pearl says, her mouth full and sleepy. "The boys."

"Disassemble," Nest says. "They unmake things. All the things that were made and not needed, they unmake so that they can become something else." I imagine cardboard boxes and exercise bikes and archaic computers.

When the girls go back to bed, I pull back the ironed curtains and look out the window at the empty yard and I make a list of the boys we used to play with. Stephen and Michael and Jonathan and Tom. And the girls. Heather and Alinya and Cassie and Megan. We played and there seemed to be no differences between them, the boys and the girls, only that we all wanted to run and hide and escape and shout and win. I know we are all doing what we are supposed to be doing now, that this is a new world that we must capture and unmake, that there are no winners but only survivors. But there is also no one left to play capture-the-flag with.

Weeks pass, and then one night moonlight finds its way through the heavy curtains. When I open them, the sky is bright and clear. I could almost imagine it blue, but vast and black is close enough. I wake the girls and bribe them with macaroni and the last of the bacon. Then we go outside. I take an ironed pillowcase and snip it in half with my shears. My husband comes out yawning, and when I give him macaroni he seems less sad. Even though there are only four of us, we make teams. Pearl picks my husband, and Nest and I take our flag and hide it in the rain barrel, which has been empty for the last four winters.

Nest guards the flag while I crawl along the ground to the other side, covering myself in moonlit dust. My husband, who was a boy once, is dozing next to the stump. I slip the flag out from where it dangles from his pocket. I run and run and run with it and no one notices me until it is too late. I love capturing so much that I take the flag back again and tuck it under my husband. Pearl sees me this time and she chases me and then Nest chases her and we laugh so loudly that it is almost as if there are boys here, and girls, too, and other people who used to be children.

My daughters' faces change in the moonlight: they look fragile, luminous, brave. They look like the children they should be. As I tuck them back in bed, their lips shiny with grease and youth, I see their school uniforms hanging on the back of the door. The badges look at me like twin eyes. I glare back. I don't care how proud the neighbors are. For my girls there should be only clear skies and running and trees, if they will ever come back again. I should be the one who does the work, who looks tired and a week older with every day that passes.

I slide the uniforms from their hangers. Through the night, I rip open seams and sew them back together. I iron, I iron. I am iron. A flashcard with Iron would have a picture of a blood cell. It would have a picture of me.

The girls are so plump with sleep that they do not notice me at first over their small bowls of cereal. Then Nest gasps. "Mom. What were you thinking?"

"This is the work I should be doing," I say. "It is my work to do, not yours." None of us recognize this voice of mine. When they laugh, I say it louder. When they stop laughing, I shout so that they can hear me over the whirring air filter. The uniform's stiff fabric feels like a shell. At least it is mine.

Finally, Nest stands up from the table and takes from my hand the spatula that I don't know I'm holding.

"It's not your work," Nest says. "Not any more. You did what you could."

"But I didn't. None of us did."

"You're right," Pearl says. My Pearl. Nest looks at her sister; there is the smallest of head shakes. "No, Mom," she says. "You can't. Besides, you hate wearing green." This is true. It reminds me too much of the world as it once was.

I sit down on the chair where Nest has been sitting. It is still warm. "I'm so good at capturing."

"Not this kind," Nest says. She sighs. Pearl scoots her chair over until it's right in front of me. She reaches out and holds my face in her cupped palms.

"You must have worked all night," my husband says, looking up from his paper. "You rest. I'll walk the girls." They find green clothes—t-shirts, sweatpants, Nest wears her father's too-large bathrobe. They are off to do the work, the work I didn't do, gathering up all the pieces of the world I didn't manage to hold onto before they were gone.

Inside, I am more restless than usual. I iron the newspaper and the rug and even my own hair. At noon, I am still wearing my patchworked green uniform, the lapels pressed to a cutting sharpness. I still have the sunburst feeling of the flag in my hand, and I let this carry me outside, into the world, and down the streets to my daughters' school.

In the school office, the two secretaries greet me with cheerful burbling. "You are the mother!" the pair of them say to me. "The mother! Oh, your daughters! Oh!" They look like a two-yolked egg, their teeth slightly yellow against their green scarves. I lick my own teeth, which feel as pointy as my lapels.

"They are so good at their work—so good. They are capturing like crazy."

"Like crazy?" I say.

"Better than crazy," the taller one says. Her hair looks as if it could capture its own planet's worth of carbon. Dense and wiry, so blonde it is almost green. The other woman's hair is a dark red-brown. Chestnut—a word my daughters only know as a color of hair. I will have to make a flashcard. I will have to make flashcards for Puffy White Clouds and Beach Umbrellas and Airplanes. I will write the script: *People once took these to other places just to see somewhere new.* Just to See the World!

"Oh yes," says the blonde one. "Their work is better than a hundred thousand planted redwood seedlings, better than dissembling a thousand cars—"

"Disassembling," the tree-haired one says. The two of them stand shoulder-to-shoulder in front of a large door, and their shoulders look as impenetrable as shopping malls.

"Better than a cow the size of the moon!" The blonde one claps her hands.

"Cows work the other way," the other secretary, the other door-guard, says. "They fart out gas."

"They fart!" We all giggle, distracted by cows.

"Like a peat bog the size of the moon?" I ask. There was a boy on my first list named Peat, spelled like the bog. His eyes were brown. He died, like so many of those boys did, before they could dissemble the bad air. So many things have gone wrong.

"Yes," the women agree. "Yes. They are so very good at capturing."

I am, too. While they are talking I capture the keys that they left swinging brightly on a hook by their desk. I take the keys and push through their shoulders and quickly unlock the doors.

"Stop, stop!" they both say. Their voices are as hopeful as words written on flashcards. I do not stop.

The doors open onto a hall, which turns into a larger hall. On the far side is an archway filled with light. I run through it and come out into a giant stadium, open to the sky. In the center of it are two enormous diving boards painted, by someone who has never seen a tree, to look like trees. There are browns and greens and yellows, but the colors are all in the wrong places.

On top of these trees are my daughters. There is no water beneath them, only Astroturf. They are so very, very high. Down in the stadium seats, there are small bunches of girls. Girls wrapped in silvery blankets, girls sprawled across each other, girls cradling each other's heads in their hands. I reach up and touch my own face the same way Pearl did this morning. There are girls lying on beds made of piles of green uniforms, with IV bags full of emerald liquid dripping into the soft insides of their arms. There are other girls sitting alone. They look the most harrowed of all.

At least my girls have each other. My girls. I look up. Each of my daughters is alone on a diving board. Each steps out toward the end of the board and grips onto the edge with her toes.

I begin to climb the rungs on the spine of the trees. As I get closer, my daughters open their mouths. Their mouths do not look like regular mouths; they are as big as undersea vents, as dark inside. Molecules shimmer around them and pour in. It is the carbon. They are capturing it. It is pouring in, purpling and iridescent like a bruise.

There is nowhere for the carbon to go once inside them. One of the girls—it is Pearl—clutches her belly and doubles over. Nest glances down at her sister. Keeping her mouth open, she reaches out a hand and circles the palm on Pearl's back. They stay like this, one standing, one crouching, their mouths still open, the carbon still pouring in.

It gets easier and easier to climb. As I climb I feel the air around me get clearer, cleaner. It is like breathing in all of spring but without the pollen, It is like popsicles and ice baths and glaciers gleaming into my lungs. It almost makes me dizzy. As I breathe, Nest starts to crumple. No, no, no—this is not how it's supposed to be. I take off my uniform jacket with one hand, holding onto the top rung with the other. I rip the fabric with my sharp teeth and wave it like a flag. "Here," I shout. "You can't get me! I've got it!" A roaring sound starts up in my ears that at first sounds like cheering. But it is only the wind beginning to pick up, echoing through the stadium. Where are the children? Where are the boys? This game only works if there is someone left who is trying to get the flag back.

MR. OCTOBER

THE DEAD MAN is running for mayor again. This happens once a year, when he comes out from the attic on the last day of September. His yard sign goes up on dirt pile on the far side of the driveway. It's bright red and says **MAYOR—WHAT THE HAL?**

Hal is the dead man's name. He likes jokes like these, puns about being dead. Every day, the alive people arrange Hal and his attic companions in the yard in a different configuration. Sometimes the alive even write dead jokes on a dry-erase board propped along the fence. Those are Hal's favorite days.

The yard sign is not handwritten: it's a real campaign yard sign. Sometimes, the alive talk about writing Hal in on the ballot though he can no longer press the flesh. He repeats this to the ghost, the zombie, the skeleton of the dog. "Can't even press the flesh!" His laugh is the sound of a dozen dice falling on a tile floor.

The alive run his campaign. First, they have him start a pet grooming business on their front lawn. They set out a folding table with the dog skeleton on top of it. They tape a set of clippers against Hal's bony hand. Instead of an election-year pun, the white board reads "Hocus Pocus Grooming." Next to the sign, the zombie walks a cat skeleton on a leash. The clippers feel solid in the dead man's hand, powerful. The dead man is good at this: the dog has no hair at all.

The next day, the alive decide that the dead man should be a short-order cook. He wears a paper hat around his skull and points at the two specials on the board: bone broth and knuckle sandwich. The only customer is the witch, who stirs the broth with a green fingernail.

One day, Hal plays golf with the vampire, the skeleton dog as his caddy. The next, he's cheering the Yankees during their wild-card game. He needs to be responsive to current events, so Hal switches his allegiance to the Dodgers in the postseason. He and his companions all wear face masks and stand next to a white board that reads THANK YOU! DOCTORS / NURSES / FIREFIGHTERS / TEACHERS. He appreciates the effort to reach a wide audience.

But by the middle of October, the dead man is tired. Before dawn, he goes down to the beach and lets the sound of the waves filter between his shin bones. The moon is still up over the hill, and everything shines: his bones, the bright masts of the boats, the water. Dolphins knife their dorsal fins up through the shine. Alive people come down to the water to watch the dolphins. For once they are so focused on life that they do not notice his bones, even as they glow pale pink in the sunrise.

Soon, the dead man is not only running for mayor, he is a superhero. The red satin cape glimmers fetchingly against his bare ribs. Yet no one asks him for help. Perhaps this is his kryptonite: no one relies on the dead man for anything. Hal feels sorry for himself for most of the day. Then he realizes he can turn this into a good answer to an interview question: *more than anything, I want to be of service.*

On the last day of October, the air seems to be full of invisible fireworks, packed with so much energy that Hal almost feels like he can breathe. He and his companions gather around the doorway: the vampire with his widow's peak, the gauze-covered ghost, another dead man who, Hal thinks, is much worse off than him. This other dead man has gray, oozy skin, and his eyes roll back as if he is in terrible pain. There is always someone who has it worse, even when they're dead.

When night falls, the children come. They are different than regular alive people. They can't vote yet, for one thing. They crowd around the doorway, the alive people inside give them food, and the air is thick with caramelized gratitude that is both saccharine and real. Some of the children even admire the dead man and his companions. Is that a tear on the zombie's face, or is it some post-mortem fluid expulsion? A few children even touch the long bones of Hal's forearm. This is what elections feel like: vibrant with possibility, not only the possibility that *his* life—or death— would change, but that somehow, he could change others' lives, too. For the better, he should make sure to emphasize.

Then the children's voices fade onto distant streets. One by one, the houses around them turn off their lights. Hal and the other dead still stand there, gathered around the door, as if waiting to conduct an exit poll. They are exhausted, exhilarated, by so much life.

The next day, the first of November, the dead man is put away in the attic with the others. He realizes they are all men, even the witch. The dead man wonders where the women are. In another attic? He hopes they made it to the polls. And what about the dead children? But no—even for a dead man, it is too hard to think of this. He hopes there are no dead children anywhere, and not just because they can't vote.

It will be eleven more months before he is unfolded again and brought down with his companions to the yard. Still, two days later, something happens. The alive shout as they watch the results—Hal has won as a write-in candidate. In the attic, the dead man presses

the three tiny bones of his middle ear to the floorboards and listens
to the people chanting HAL HAL HAL. For a moment, the house
feels as if it is made of water. His name in their living mouths makes
the sound of the waves hitting rocks, then tumbling back toward
the sea.

PIE TIN

THE FIRST PIE TIN I bought was my least favorite. Stainless steel and so shiny that it sometimes hurt to look at. I wanted a tin that was less reflective, more like the ones Bea had. She bought them cheap and tarnished from the resale shop so that if they didn't come back, she wouldn't miss them. I went to the same shop, and the shiny pie tin sat there as if marveling in its own newness among all the rusty egg beaters and spatulas and sheet pans. For a long time, it was the only pie tin I had.

It was the tin that kept coming back—how many times, I didn't know—even though the dull metal ones I accumulated later disappeared. The shiny tin sat on the kitchen counter next to the window, where a small corner of sky mirrored itself in the flat bottom. Scratch marks in the stainless steel from knives and forks cut across the blue reflection of the sky, carving the sky into quarters, eighths. Maybe just one more piece to even it out.

If this were another kind of story, the tin I hated would have been a magic pie tin that filled and refilled itself with pie so that no one would ever go hungry. But it's not that kind of story. In this one, people's mouths fill with mud and they never eat pie again.

Egyptians likely made the earliest pies: free-for-all mixes of grains and honey, then bread dough filled with fruit and nuts. Then there were the sturdy-crusted pies, so tough no tin was needed. They were called coffins if they had a lid. They were called traps if they didn't. Sometimes, they could stand up on their own for days.

I did not grow up eating pie. Instead I got to know pies through nursery rhymes and picture books, thought of them as cages for blackbirds and the mystery location of Lowly Worm's hat. I always felt so sad and strange about the blackbirds. I imagined the texture of feathers in my mouth, the crunch of the smallest of bones. I wondered if the king had to pretend to smile with bits of black featherdown leaking out of the corners of his mouth.

I was relieved, then, when I learned that the birds probably weren't eaten. Pies like that were meant to delight. Cut open the coffin and you'd find singing birds, birds that could even fly up and out an open window. Pies once contained live animals, even people. One enormous pie had a filling of 28 musicians and their instruments. There is no record of what they played. Pie songs, maybe, melodies of savory and sweet.

I started making pie because of Bea. She lived up the street and took care of babies in a house like a fairytale cottage with tiny reading nooks and wooden walls painted with ivy and big-eyed forest animals. Every Thanksgiving she baked an apple pie for each family in her care. One time she baked a pie for me, too, even though I had no babies. I took the pie on a camping trip to Yosemite. When it started snowing, I scrambled to find a hotel, where I ate the whole pie as I sat on the queen-sized bed, watching the Thanksgiving Day Parade. I felt like I'd never eaten pie before. This is going to sound too sentimental, but it really did taste like love. Love disguised as butter and sugar and apples and cinnamon.

I asked Bea if she would teach me. Her pies were traps—no top crust, just a dusting of butter and sugar. She shaped small hearts out of leftover dough and put them on top. As we made pies together on her yellow kitchen table I felt both exhausted and refreshed, as if we'd been for a long ocean swim before coming into her kitchen. It was a Saturday, and there was no sign of the babies beyond the miniature wooden beds where they slept. Sunlight eased through the vines outside her kitchen window. Beyond them, down at the far end of our street, was the sea.

When we were done, Bea drove me half a block home in her powder blue Oldsmobile. I held a pair of warm pies on my lap. She told me I could keep the tins. I gave them back, clean and empty, but when all I could find for myself at first was the shiny tin, I wished I hadn't.

That year I baked and baked. Pies seems to bloom out of my palms. Chess and pecan, blueberry and apricot, key lime, lemon merengue. No matter how many times I tried, the apple pie always tasted the best. While the pies baked, I sat on the kitchen counter and played my mandolin.

I bought more pie tins. Almost all of them disappeared and didn't come back. I thought that this was a good thing. I peeled more apples. I bulk-ordered sugar and flour. Now there was no time to play the mandolin, only enough time to wipe the flour off the counter and begin again. I had many pie tins now, but only the shiny one kept returning clean and empty. Maybe people returned this one because they saw the same thing I did when I looked into the bottom—a reflection of their own faces.

Then the fire came. Not a kitchen fire, although I'd set off the smoke alarm multiple times as the butter bubbled and spilled over the tins and burned on the oven floor. This time, power crackled in the dry trees and a real fire started. This time, the sirens did not stop when I waved my hands in the air. The fire sprinted up hillsides and through the back doors of homes, an uninvited guest. The air turned thick and orange and dripped ash on car windows, fine as snow.

One night, the flames outlined the ridge in volcanic glory. We were supposed to be inside. It was supposed to be winter, when there were no fires. And then, as if by miracle, which was the same thing as many people working together for days on end, the fire was out, and real winter came. I stopped baking. I didn't want smoke inside after all that had surrounded us.

With winter came rain. At first, the tree-stripped hills ran dark with clumps of small rocks and slipping dirt. But the rain stopped. The dirt stopped. Everyone sighed. Then the rain returned, hitting the roof hard and fast. There were so many things between the rain and me—the beams, the attic, the brick-like storage boxes, the plaster of the ceiling. Still, I could feel the force of the water on my own skin.

The hillsides felt it, too. A mile away, boulders swept through the creek beds and bowled themselves into houses. Mud poured into kitchens and bedrooms. There was quiet after the rain stopped. Then more silence. Then the thump of helicopter blades. At first there was no news, and then there was too much of it.

A mile away, people were trapped and buried in hardening mud. Without thinking, I cut butter into small pieces and worked it into the flour, digging, digging. What other option did I have? I took the shiny tin and covered over my reflection with dough, so that I couldn't see the face of someone who did not know how to help.

Bea told me anytime you use flour and butter and sugar, you can't go wrong. I went wrong. My pie kept getting bigger. I let the crust overflow from the pie tin, I spackled it together to make it higher and wider and put it in the oven. The rain started up again. I watched the droplets roll down the windows and checked weather forecasts and storm warnings.

I had forgotten about the pie in the oven. This one didn't smoke, but the crust was so thick I had to use a chainsaw to cut it. The apples inside had barely cooked.

There were still people in the mudslide, packed tight into the earth. There were still houses filled entirely with mud. There were children who, if this were a fairytale, might emerge again in a hundred years to find a new and different world, where it was everyone else, and not them, who had died. I tried to make another pie. When I lifted the lid of the sugar jar, I found there were only a few crystals left, forming a rime around the bottom.

I walked up the hill to Bea's and knocked on her door. From inside, she called out that I should come in. She was in the kitchen. There were babies everywhere. One baby sat in a chair, and another crawled across the rug holding a whisk in one hand. A third baby closed a cupboard over and over. A slightly bigger baby stood holding onto the leg of Bea's yellow table. The baby toddled over to a drawer and took out all of the plastic bowls inside.

Bea did not seem worried. She was holding a baby on one hip. I asked to borrow some sugar. Instead, Bea handed the baby to me. "I'm running out of things, too," she said. She asked the baby slamming the cupboard if she could look inside. The baby in my arms leaned its head against me. It smelled like just-baked bread. In the yard beyond the kitchen door, a small girl used one of Bea's pie tins to scoop up mud from a puddle.

"Here," Bea said. She handed me a jar of wooden clothespins and took the baby out of my arms. "These might work." Outside, the little girl with the pie tin now patted the mud into place and sprinkled flower petals on the surface.

My arms felt empty, even though I held the clothespins. Everywhere felt empty, even though there were still babies all around. "What do I do?" I asked.

Bea shifted from side to side, and the baby that had just been in my arms closed its eyes. "He's asleep," she said. "Everything can become something else if you need it to be."

At home, I set the clothespins on the counter next to the shiny pie tin. I made another crust. This one was so thick that my rolling pin hardly made a dent in it. Instead I pulled it into the shape of a bowl with my hands. I had no sugar, so I filled this one with plain apples and cinnamon. I made another crust, even bigger, then another. When the apples ran out, I kept making crusts. I made only coffins now, a lid of crust on top of a pie with nothing inside.

A friend came over for a cup of tea. We sat at the table, where I'd set all of the crusts. Some were the size of large pizzas. One was as round and puffy as an inner tube. "It's just a few miles away," we said to each other. "We feel so helpless." The sky through the window now overflowed with sunshine. I didn't dare to look in the shiny tin on the counter, where the blue reflection would seem even more cruel.

I told my friend I couldn't even make real pies anymore. She poked at one of the empty pie crusts with a fork before giving up. Instead, she picked up the crust and nibbled at it until it was gone. "That didn't taste helpless," she said.

That night I mixed ingredients in the bathtub. I pulled the doors off my car and hammered them into a larger tin. The solar panels on the roof, angled just right, cooked the crust into brick. The pie was strong enough to float, so I took it down to the water and towed it behind my kayak. We went across the soupy mix of waves next to the harbor's breakwater, past the buoys and the wharf, all the way to the outlet of the creek that was littered with timbers and garbage and the clothes that the force of the flooding creeks had stripped from people's bodies.

I landed and the pie thumped onto the beach behind me. I held out forks to the people who stood there in their muddy boots. They set down their buckets and shovels, but they were too sad to eat.

What could I do? I made another crust, even bigger. The whole neighborhood came out to watch me spread a paste of butter and flour on the cracking sides. I made it so strong that no rising water could break it. I made a flag from a white pillowcase and attached it to the crust with the wooden clothespins, so that this pie could become something that might help.

I found my mandolin and climbed inside. I brought the shiny pie tin, too—it looked so small now, and somehow I couldn't leave it all alone on the counter, reflecting empty skies back to no one. It was the one, I realized, that I would miss.

My neighbors loaded the top of the pie onto the crust with a small crane. Bea was there, too. There was a scratching sound above me: she was using the edge of a shovel to trace out a pair of hearts, each the size of her body.

The crust shifted and sighed as my neighbors lowered it into the water, but it did not dissolve. The wind carried the two of us, me and the crust, to the east. To pass the time I played "Dueling Banjos," both parts. Then I played "Rainbow Connection," and "It's a Wonderful World," and "Both Sides Now." I played every song that I could think of about the sky so that, if anyone down in the mud could still hear, the melody might tell them that somewhere, it was still blue. I wanted the smell of butter and sugar to drift inland and call them out of the mud, even if only so that people could find their bodies and know for sure.

Through the crack in the coffin lid I could see a fracture line of sky along the edge of one of the hearts. I set down the mandolin and picked up the empty pie tin. I turned it away from me, letting the shine of it send light back out through the crack. There was a bump. Maybe we had found solid ground at last.

FOR LIA, WHO WANTED TO FLY

THE LAST BEAUTIFUL THING Jesse remembered from the night Lia died was crossing the street and startling a flock of pigeons out of a tree. The pigeons careened through his peripheral vision, their dark bodies speckling the greyed-out tule fog that marked winter evenings in Sacramento. Then Jesse felt something wet drip off his hair onto the electric skin just above his collar, the place where he'd imagined Lia kissing him. He stalked home and showered off the pigeon shit and got into bed. The clean feeling bled into the slight grime of his Star Wars sheets, which he wished he'd agreed to let his mom wash.

The next thing he remembered was his mom kneeling by his bed. Her hand peeled back his sweaty hair from his forehead. The light through the windows was still grey, but it carried an oranger hue that meant it was well past midnight, all streetlight with no memory of the sun. "Can you wait to wash my sheets until morning?" Jesse mumbled. He turned over to get away from her hand.

"Thank God," his mother said. "You're safe." That's when he turned back over to squint at her streaky face. Her mouth trembled like she'd just seen a miracle turned inside out. Like the time the

Silver Surfer rescued a baby flung into a volcano, only to have it turn into a monster in his arms. It was a pivotal issue, #34, the same one where Thanos gets resurrected before he sets out to destroy half the universe.

Then he started to hear what his mother was saying. *There was an accident. Some kids were driving drunk. And Lia—*

Thank God you're ok, she said at last. Jesse closed his eyes and wished that he had been with Lia so that he didn't have to know the rest.

Jesse's dad had built the treehouse in the walnut tree next to the back fence the year the Bonifaces moved in to the house behind their own. Jesse and the Bonifaces' older daughter, Lia, were the only second-graders in town that did not play soccer on Saturday mornings. Jesse had his asthma. Lia went to the first day of practice with her new team and came home saying she never wanted to play soccer again.

So Jesse's dad and Lia's dad built a trapdoor to the treehouse and a rope ladder that led up from Lia's backyard so that the two of them could go from house to house without walking around the block. The far side of the block was Land Park Drive, a road that their parents didn't think it was safe to walk on—too many teenagers driving too fast. So Lia climbed up from her yard, and Jesse climbed up from his.

On Saturdays Lia's mom would send her with juice boxes and sandwiches—peanut butter and jelly for Lia, peanut butter and banana for Jesse—and the two of them would sit in the treehouse and read Jesse's comics. Later in the morning, Jesse's mom would hand up toaster waffles and orange slices. Their own halftime snack. The oranges were ones that Jesse's family bought from the Boniface family produce market, where Lia helped her dad make fresh-squeezed orange juice and pour it into bottles. Even when she washed her hands over and over, the smell of oranges never quite went away.

Inside the treehouse Jesse had shelves for his action figures and his comics. Lia brought an old baby quilt and bottles that she filled with acorns and rocks and bottle caps. Her dad handed up milk crates from the market. They sat on the crates or used them to set up scenes with Jesse's figures and Lia's treasures, which included an abalone shell that Lia's aunt had brought her from the coast. The shell became a base, a jail, and sometimes, the chariot of Aquaman or the Silver Surfer's board, the inner surface turning pewter or iridescent, depending on how the light hit it.

On Jesse's side of the treehouse there was a tire swing. Lia's side had a zipline and a set of hanging rings and Lia's sister, Katy, who sometimes played with Jesse and Lia if they descended into the yard. Mostly they stayed in the treehouse and talked. Jesse would tell Lia what was happening in the issue he was reading, while Lia arranged her treasures or wove friendship bracelets that were safety-pinned to the leg of her jeans. Sometimes she would wrap her quilt around her legs and look up through the skylight that Jesse's dad had cut out of the plywood.

She made Jesse a bracelet once, a band of blue and yellow chevrons that she tied around his wrist. "Is it blue and gold for the X-Men or—" He thought for a moment. "The Aggies?" His dad would be proud, he took Jesse and Lia to a basketball game at UC Davis once and, look, Jesse had remembered the name of the team.

"I liked the colors together," Lia said. "I thought you would like it."

"I do," he said, relieved. "You know, Blue Diamond is blue and yellow. He's got a diamond embedded in his body that makes him as strong and tough as a diamond. Although, I don't know, I guess I'd rather be the Flash. He's red and yellow." If he was the Flash, he could run fast enough to play soccer. He could run as fast as Lia, who sprinted across the playground faster than anyone, the colored barrettes on her ponytails a metronome of clicks. Wheezy earthling Jesse could never keep up with her. "Who would you be?" he asked.

"Wonder Woman," she said. "Except."

"Except what?" Lia didn't answer. Jesse shrugged. "She's boring anyway."

"I don't look like her," Lia said. She was on her back now, the quilt over her stomach, watching the sky.

He peered at Lia. She looked like she always did, like herself, glasses and braided hair and a dimple on her left cheek when she smiled. "I don't look like Flash," Jesse said. Jesse looked like his father, a skinny, pale accountant with a halo of frizzy brown hair.

"Okay, give me some ideas then."

Jesse thought. "What about Storm? She can control the weather, she has magic, she can pick locks. You could make it not so hot. Or Captain Marvel—she can convert her body to energy." Jesse started to pull out back issues.

Lia shook her head. "I want to fly," she said. "Give me one that can fly."

"Bumblebee," he said. "Captain Marvel, too."

"That sounds weak," she said. "And isn't Bumblebee tiny?"

"She's not weak. She made herself a suit so she can fly. Bumblebee can do a lot, even though she's small."

"I don't want to be small," Lia said. She sat up and collected threads for a new bracelet. She tied them together on a safety pin and tethered the pin to her jeans. She'd showed Jesse how to do it once but he couldn't follow. "But you should be Flash. And I'll be the one who knows your secret identity, and I'll cover for you when you have to go off and be a hero." Lia paused and licked the tips of her fingers. She pressed down on the ends of the threads where they had frayed. Then she looped them all into a knot to hold her place. "Let's go on the zipline. I want to see if I can throw a water balloon when I'm on it. Wouldn't that be great to get Katy?" Lia's sister Katy was alternately the victim of any trick they could come up with and a valued asset when it came to games that required more than two people. Katy seemed to be able to understand this better than Jesse, who was an only child.

Jesse followed her down the rope ladder on her side. In the yard, Lia's younger sister was nowhere to be seen as they filled water balloons, stretching the thin skin around the faucet bib. The September sun through the walnut leaves turned everything green and watery. Maybe he should be Aquaman, he thought, even though he hated the water. Because when the light was like this and he was with Lia, he could be anything.

The morning after Lia died Jesse sat in the treehouse and stared through the cut-out skylight. At seventeen, his body felt cramped and awkward inside the plywood walls. Neither he nor Lia had taken care of the treehouse the past few years. The skylight now showed warbled views of walnut leaves and a too-blue sky that seemed not to realize everything was now terrible.

Jesse had moved his comics inside long ago—some of them were collectibles by then, and now he knew better than to leave them out in the sun and rain. Still, he thought more of Lia's things would still be here. There were a few old bottles and the pair of pale-blue milk crates. Her quilt wasn't anywhere. His throat hurt. He wanted something that would smell like Lia, something he could bury his face into and disappear. When Jesse went back inside to get an ibuprofen for his throat, he saw his father's electric clippers sitting in the hall closet. He plugged the clippers in and blazed a line down the center of his head. Then another and another, until all the hair was gone. His throat still hurt. Maybe it was the pollen.

After the funeral, he hugged Mrs. Boniface's narrow shoulders and shook Mr. Boniface's hand. Their faces were stiff as tree bark. "Why weren't you the one driving, Jesse?" Mr. Boniface asked. "You always drove Lia everywhere."

"Hush," Mrs. Boniface said to her husband. "It's not his fault."

Mr. Boniface didn't sound angry, just deeply confused. Then

Jesse's father stepped around Jesse and wrapped Mr. Boniface in a hug, looking both small and much more powerful than Lia's enormous father.

Jesse drifted away from the Bonifaces and his parents, who were now all hugging each other and weeping, their faces suddenly looking much less solid than trees, becoming more like old buildings that crumbled down under their own weight.

For a few weeks, it felt like the hallways at school were holding their breath. Then Jesse heard about a party out in Elk Grove at Manny Pacheco's stepmother's house, a tract home in one of the new developments. At first he seethed—how could anyone have a party after what happened with Lia? But somehow he couldn't maintain the energy that rage required. Besides, what else was he going to do?

Flags waved along the freshly-paved street as if a medieval jousting tournament was being held inside. Jesse parked down the block and found his way inside. He sat down on a beanbag chair in the corner of the living room without saying hello to anyone and watched the tide of the party rise around him.

Three junior girls sat queen-like on the kitchen island with their ponytails and red cups and sophomore peasants gathering around their feet. Manny Pacheco was there, too, laughing so hard that his face turned pink. Manny's cheeks were as smooth as a girl's. The acne that clustered around Jesse's nose started to pulse with resentment. He pushed himself off the beanbag chair. His nose itched. He wiped at it with the back of his shirtsleeve and sneezed. A dog bed. He'd been sitting in a dog bed.

No one noticed Jesse get up. They were too busy drinking, which was exactly what Lia must have been doing the last time she was alive. Not that much—she never would have had that much, Jesse knew how she was. Lia liked the weight of the bottle dangling from her fingers. She liked the sensation of being tipsy, liked the word *tipsy*. She would have said it, over and over, to anyone who would listen, even though she would have had only about three ounces of the wine cooler or whatever it was that Nathan Ruskey had probably given her and the other two girls in the car with him. *Tipsy tipsy tipsy.* The rest of them had only been bruised, but Lia had flown from the car and into a tree along Land Park, a few blocks from home.

Jesse's hands went up to his own head, as if trying to protect it, as if somehow he could have cradled Lia's head before it hit the tree. His fingers brushed the fuzz of hair that was already coming up around his temples.

Lia had teased him about his hair at the beginning of summer, when he came up into the treehouse and found Lia and another girl up there. The two girls were wearing red lipstick, which looked like molten lava on Lia and like scary blood on the other girl. The backs of their hands were covered with flower-like smears.

"Are you practicing kissing?" Jesse had asked.

"Jesse Aldridge is your backyard neighbor," the other girl said, her voice a shovelful of boredom.

"He's my best friend," Lia said. "Go away, Jesse."

Jesse had crept backward down the ladder. His chest felt like it was bare and being hit with the warmest rays of sun.

"Jesse!" Lia shouted. "I know you're standing on the last rung still, you're shaking the whole tree. I can see your nasty man-perm."

"It's not a perm! I grew this myself!" Jesse shouted back. He stepped off the ladder onto the grass, waiting.

"I can still hear your mouth-breathing. Go away, Jesse!"

Jesse took in a big breath of air and closed his mouth. The air blazed in his lungs. He had been deliriously happy then, standing in the yard, shouting with Lia.

Now he rubbed his hands over his head as he went outside and tried to make it through the crowd to the keg by the barbeque. He wondered if anyone recognized him without his hair. Maybe some girls would want to touch his head and take pity on him.

But no. No one even looked at him. The only person who had noticed his hair was his mother, who had tucked the corner of her lip beneath her cockeyed front teeth and worked hard at not crying. "Don't cry about my hair," he had said. "It's just hair."

"I'm not crying about your hair," she said.

And then he wished she had been.

Nathan Ruskey certainly didn't notice him, although the boy had been in Jesse's peripheral vision from the moment Jesse stepped into the backyard. Nathan was now at the far side of the bean-shaped pool, lit turquoise and tropical even though they were in the middle of nowhere. It was as if Nathan was tagged by some radioactive material that only Jesse could see, glowing bright and more insistent every time Jesse turned his head. Nathan was surrounded by girls—getting him drinks, nodding sympathetically, taking turns rubbing Nathan's shoulders through a thin, too-tight t-shirt. Nuclear unfairness. Jesse knew he would have to do something eventually, otherwise he might explode.

Lia had been obsessed with Nathan Ruskey, ever since the boy—why did he look so much like a man already?—came to their school halfway through freshmen year. Lia had helped organize the protest for the Gulf War that year. She'd passed out flyers! She had glow-in-the-dark peace signs painted on her jeans! The night before, when Jesse had told her how worried he was about walking out of class, she told him to sack up and show up. But when he looked for her out on the quad, his heart pounding with fear and excitement, he hadn't seen her.

Jesse had found Lia after school that day on the quad, waiting for her dad to pick both of them up. "Where were you?" he asked. "One of the seniors got naked and wrapped a flag around himself. I don't even think he's getting detention."

She shrugged. "Nathan Ruskey said he wasn't going to go, that we needed to support the troops. His dad's at the air force base." She shrugged. "Besides, it's kind of cool he doesn't follow the crowd. Most people went so they could miss class." Just as Jesse was about to deflate, she had looked right at him. "Not you," she said. "I know you went for both of us." Jesse's heart had swelled. And Lia had been following Nathan Ruskey around ever since.

Lia tried out for the swim team because that's what Nathan Ruskey did. She'd made it on the JV team, which practiced after school. The varsity team, which of course—*of course*—Nathan Ruskey was on, practiced at dawn. After a few weeks, Lia told her parents that she wasn't going to be on the team after all, because she was worried her schoolwork would suffer. "The girls are lame," she had told Jesse. But Jesse knew it was Nathan Ruskey. Lia always called him by his whole name, *Nathan Ruskey.*

"You fucker," Jesse said now, looking at the boy on the other side of the fake lawn. Jesse abandoned the line for the keg and began pushing his way through college sweatshirts and baseball caps and the smell of cheap cologne. He knew it was Calvin Klein Obsession, he had that kind, too. He got a bottle of it with his tutoring money after Lia said she liked how Nathan Ruskey smelled.

Jesse was now so intent on reaching Nathan he didn't see who bumped into him. "Sorry," he said, continuing to walk. Someone shouldered him again, this time so hard that he spun around and veered sideways toward a camelia bush. He blinked and looked around, lamely patting his own shoulder, which felt tender. He found himself in a dark part of the yard, next to some trash cans. "Hey, fuck you," he said to the darkness. He tried to say it loudly, without sounding scared about who would answer.

"Ooo, Jess. So tough."

Now it wasn't just his shoulder that hurt, it was his brain, because he'd know Lia's voice anywhere.

"Don't look so stupid. Of course it's me," Lia said. "Who else would it be?"

Jesse stepped away from the voice, backing toward a window that was framed in tiny lights shaped like red chili peppers. The pinkish glow lit her from behind. It did look like Lia, although she was wearing something weird—weirder, anyway, than her usual cut-off jeans and striped socks and leather Jesus sandals, or polka-dot pajama bottoms during school, or sundresses late at night during winter. Not that he had noticed.

Now Lia had on tall boots that came up over her knees and something that looked like a tinfoil crown and a t-shirt with a symbol, drawn in Magic Marker, on the front. He tried to skim his eyes over the symbol, which was the same place her breasts were. There was a ragged piece of fabric draped across her back.

"I *know*," she said. "I'm still working on it."

Jesse glanced around. No one seemed to be looking at either of them, here at the side of the house with the trash cans and the capsaicin glow. "What are you supposed to be, exactly?" he asked

She rolled her eyes and looked over his shoulder. "I'm a superhero. You're the one who should know that." Jesse stepped closer to her. She grabbed his shoulder and moved him out of the way so that she could gaze beyond him into the crowd. Jesse winced. Bruises like grapes were already sprouting on the skin underneath his sweatshirt.

"I don't get it," he said, rubbing his shoulder. "Aren't you dead?" To his relief, this caught her attention. "You know, the League doesn't get it, either."

"So you're DC then," Jesse said. "Not Marvel."

Lia waved a hand at him, as if to brush aside this mortal nonsense. "They're thinking it was something related to the crash—you know, the tree I got thrown into was radioactively contaminated, or it amplified particularly strong cosmic rays. Apparently there was a solar flare at the same time."

Maybe he was dead, too, although that didn't make sense either—his heart chugged along inside his ribs, picked up speed. "So," he asked, "what makes you so super?" He could list them himself, a million things.

"What doesn't?" she asked. But then she climbed up on top of one of the trash cans and scaled a trellis covered in rose-colored roses. She was on the roof before he could remember to breathe. Then she did a backflip—a backflip!—and the air around her coagulated to slow her fall. Lia hovered in front of him for a moment, then stepped down to the ground as if emerging from an invisible carriage. Her boots, trimmed with duct tape, didn't make a sound on the Astroturf lawn.

"Holy crap, Lia."

"Let's go," Lia said.

Anywhere. Should he step into her arms so that she could fly off with him, or would that be too embarrassing? Would the crowds part and people fall down around them in awe? Or maybe they'd throw rose petals, or Mardi Gras beads. Would anyone take off their shirts? Lia's hand, warm and whole, threaded its way through his.

Jesse froze. What else do you do when you have everything you ever wanted? "Come *on*, Jesse. I need your help," Lia said. "Nathan Ruskey is right over there."

This is it, Jesse thought. Nathan Ruskey killed Lia, or at least, made her die, which was almost the same thing; now the two of them were going to kill Nathan Ruskey. "Nice hair, by the way," Lia said, and then she pulled Jesse forward.

If this is what being dead is like, Jesse thought, I love it already.

The crowd did part as they moved. But people seemed to back away from them as if they didn't see Lia and Jesse passing through. A trio of football players got shuffled off to one side, still bent over someone's GameBoy. The girls from the volleyball team, all high ponytails and legs, were eased toward the house. Their bright voices didn't stop.

"I can help a little. You know I've done aikido forever," Jesse said to Lia. Jesse had started doing martial arts after the same kid kept throwing pencils at his head in fourth grade. Lia knew this. What she didn't know was that in the last few months, Jesse felt as if he were finally growing into his body, the geometry of elbows and knees and shoulders working together even though everything else had stopped making sense.

"What?" Lia stopped and looked right at him. Her face had the shape and downy hair of a peach, the white part of her eyes so clear against the dark moon of iris.

"Nathan Ruskey." Jesse pointed across the parted crowd, to where a boy with a stupid floppy hat was sitting on a lawn chair next to the pool. A girl in a bikini top and cutoffs sat on Nathan's lap. "What if you do a huge bounding jump and land on the top part of the chair, so that it flips him over? Then I'll get in a *shomen uchi* and then you do whatever you want with him. Are you going to kill him or just maybe paralyze him? Then he'd have to live with the consequences."

Lia moved so fast that it seemed to make everything go on rewind, the crowd re-magnetizing around him so that he couldn't see what happened next. When he finally emerged, the girl who had been on Nathan's lap was in the pool. Five different guys flipped their ball caps backward and lurched to the water's edge to help. Nathan Ruskey sat on the lawn chair, his head in his hands. And there was Lia, standing behind him, rubbing his shoulders.

Maybe this was part of her plan. She would get Nathan relaxed, then bring on the massacre. Jesse crossed to the low shed that hummed with the pool's electrical gear. He hauled himself up on top of the shed roof and sat to wait. And wait.

Finally, he couldn't take it anymore. "Just kill him already!" he yelled at her. Then something whacked him hard on the side of the head. The air whistled near his ear. Jesse tried to duck, and in the process tumbled off the shed. He cowered on the ground as Lia stood over him, swinging a pool noodle. "Stop that," he said.

"Stop that!" Lia's voice mimicked his own, how it had cracked between the two words, low and then too high. Jesse covered his head with his hands and waited, but another blow didn't come. He sat up, still using his hands to protect his head. Lia had discarded the pool noodle and was now sitting on Nathan's lap. Nathan stared out over the pool, his eyes narrowed as if trying to read an eye chart from a million miles away.

Jesse couldn't watch. He couldn't not watch. But nothing changed. "Lia," he said at last, "does he even know you're there?" Lia stood up. She circled around the pool chair, blowing in Nathan's ear, ruffling his hair. The boy didn't move.

Her boots scuffed the ground as she returned to where Jesse sat next to the pool shed. She plopped down next to him and set her chin in her hands. "You'll help me figure this out," she said. "You know everything about superheroes."

"I don't want to help you," Jesse said.

"Oh, come on," Lia said. "So you love me. So get over it. Sorry that I had to die to tell you that."

"Why didn't you?"

"Does it help at all?"

Jesse's throat sealed up. His hands rubbed at the prickles on his head, smoothing the hairs in one direction, then the other. It did nothing. He loved her still.

Lia lowered herself on to her belly. Her impossibly strong hands pulled up clumps of plastic grass from the Astroturf. She wove strands of them together into something that looked like a nest, or a rug. Jesse crawled forward to look at what she was making. She shrugged at him, tossed the small bundle up into the air above them. It catapulted higher and higher, seeming to gain speed as it rose. "Look," someone shouted, "a shooting star!"

The night that Lia died, Jesse had refused to drive Lia to a party—a different kid's house, a different parent out of town—

because she told him that she didn't need a ride back. She was going to leave with Nathan Ruskey.

"How do you *know*?" he had asked.

"I just do," she said. "Jesse, we're a thing—or at least, we're about to be. "

"You and Nathan? No. Not even," he said. His laugh sounded like a dying duck, even to himself, even on a good day. "You're too—"

"Too what?" Her arms folded across her chest. They had been standing out in front of her house, Friday after school. The treehouse looked small from there, like a bird's nest, something fragile and impossible and empty.

"Too young," Jesse said. "And he only dates swimmers. You're not a swimmer."

"I don't think this is about how well I can swim, Jesse. Are you going to tell me what you really mean?"

"I'm not going to take you, not if you're just using me for a ride to hook up."

"It's never bothered you before."

Jesse's stomach dropped out through his pant leg. Had he taken her somewhere to hook up with Nathan and not even known it? He reeled back through all the places he'd driven her—the movies, the drive-through on Saturday nights, sometimes just along the river roads, back and forth, both of them complaining that there's nowhere to go, nothing fun to do, even though driving through the dusk with the willows tipping away from them, Lia at his side, made the inside of Jesse's throat hum. They had driven along those roads after she failed her first chemistry test but before she'd told her parents. They'd driven those roads all the way to Stockton to get Mother's Day presents and see *Point Break*, which Lia said was the stupidest movie ever even though she cried through the final scene when Keanu Reeves unlocked Patrick Swayze's handcuffs so that he could meet his fate surfing the waves of a 50-year storm. Lia was so wrecked that Jesse was the one who bought the ceramic hen that Lia wanted to get for her mom. He could remember Lia holding the hen in her hands and peering at it as they cruised past Discovery Bay, over the Old River Bridge. "She just loves chickens," Lia had said. "I have no idea why. I mean, they're not even cute. They're like little feathered reptiles." Jesse had started clucking then, and she had started clucking, and they cackled and peeped and cock-a-doodle-dooed all the way home.

But standing in front of Lia's house he had said nothing, swallowing, wishing he had never heard of Nathan Ruskey. Finally, Lia did: "That's the problem, Jesse. You haven't been paying attention."

A high-octane shame lit up inside Jesse and propelled him away from her, down the sidewalk, his Converse slapping as he ran. Now they were well past old enough to walk around the block by themselves without their parents worrying about Land Park Drive, which now seemed so quiet, so annoyingly pleasant. He ran all the way home. He'd always paid attention to her, always, but somehow, like everything else, he'd been doing it wrong.

Still, he couldn't bear to stay in his own house that night with the buzzing sound inside him that drowned out whatever he was feeling. He rode his bike around town and eventually, once it got dark, to the party. Jesse stood outside, propped up against the frame of the Schwinn, hearing the buzz from the backyard on the sidewalk, wanting to lean into the sound as if it could catch him. He told himself he could hear Lia's laugh, even though the jumble of voices was far too loud for him to distinguish any single voice, even the one that was the compass rose on the map of his cowardly heart.

He stood there for as long as he could until he started to feel creepy, and then he walked his bike home and pigeons crapped on his head and then Lia died and he couldn't say he was sorry. He couldn't say what he really meant to say, which was also probably the wrong thing: that she was too much *his* to ever be Nathan Ruskey's, even though she never had been Jesse's at all.

"What happened?" Jesse asked her now, the party a carousel around them. They were both lying back on the fake grass now, people giving them room without looking down at them. "To us, I mean."

"We changed," she said. "You can still go back there, you know, to that place where we were little. It's a real place, even if it's only a memory. I can see that now." She sighed, a wetter sound that he remembered, and then she rolled away from him. "But it wasn't a place I could stay, even if I wanted to." She was quiet for a long time. Then, even though he couldn't see her face, he had the feeling that her smile was growing toward him, weed-like, through the grass. "I didn't have a license, and you were so fun to ride with. You really were, Jesse. You are."

He shut his eyes and pressed the heels of his hands into his eyeballs. "Now that you're a superhero, it won't matter that you never got your license."

"Screw you," she said, without enthusiasm.

"I mean, that licenses aren't actually important. You know that now."

"Nothing is actually important. You know that most superheroes are nihilistic, right? I mean, they don't want the greater good. They just can't stop themselves from doing what they know how to do. Besides," she said, "I can't really fly."

This made Jesse sit up. "Really?"

Lia rolled onto her feet—if only he could have taken her to aikido, she'd have been amazing!—and walked over to the house. She grabbed onto a drainpipe and climbed, hand over hand, until she stood at the corner of the roof. Jesse's breath gathered into a fist. Then Lia stepped off. She cascaded downward and alighted on the grass next to him. "Going down is fine. I just can't get anywhere up." As if to demonstrate, she jumped off the ground. She returned to Earth just like he would, only with a little more grace.

"Maybe try pointing your arms. You know, like Superman." Jesse put his arms straight out over his head. There was laughter around them. Over by the trashcans, Ben Cooper, who graduated two years ago but still showed up at every party, was doing a keg stand. The air throbbed with people chanting his name.

"Please," Lia said. "It's not like his arms *do* anything. He's not a bird. I mean, really." She sniffed at the air, glancing around. "I wish I could smoke, but I can't even smell it. That's the thing, everything's a little bit like clouds. That's why I can do all these things. It's not hard to move fast or glide or see things when there's really nothing there. But it makes it hard to hold on to anything."

"I can feel you," Jesse said. He reached his hand out to catch hers. She squeezed it tentatively, and he realized she was trying not to hurt him this time. "Why is that?"

"I don't know," she said. "You always did make even the worst things better." She turned away, scanning the crowd. "I wish that had been enough."

Eventually, Lia went over to the diving board and began to bounce up and down on its far edge. Each time she bounced, she soared up a little higher. But still there was something that stopped her, that made Lia come to the zenith of flight, pause, and then descend again. Behind him, Jesse could hear another kegstand starting: *Man-ny! Man-ny! Man-ny!* They should be chanting for Lia. They should see her like he did. But they couldn't. Something trapped her here, invisible.

So Jesse did the only thing he could think of. He pushed himself off the ground and went and punched Nathan Ruskey on the high, sharp ridge of his beautiful cheekbone.

It hurt. Jesus, did it ever hurt. Jesse shook his hand out, blowing on his knuckles, as if that might help. Maybe aikido wasn't such a dumb sport after all, Jesse thought. You fell so that you didn't hurt yourself. He remembered to stand in ready position now, he aligned his head, his spine, and his hips with each other and with gravity. His big toes pressed into the ground through the soles of his Cons.

But Nathan stayed where he ended up, sprawled sideways on the lawn chair. He held his cheek with one hand. Girls appeared out of nowhere and clustered around him. "What did you do *that* for?" said one girl, all violet eyeshadow and outrage. Jesse stood there, ready, until it was clear that nothing else would happen. The crowd filled in around him again as if he didn't exist. He couldn't see Lia anywhere.

Jesse took himself to the edge of the pool and lowered himself in. The water filtered into his jeans slowly and then all at once. He leaned his head back against the side of the pool, looking up at the sky, looking for Lia. The diving board was still.

"Hey. Hey. Hey, man," a voice said. Jesse tipped his head to the side a little, the concrete edge of the pool grinding into the back of his neck.

"What?" he said. Someone squatted down and took off their shoes and put their feet in the water. Big feet. Enormous. They almost look webbed. Was it Aquaman? At this point, he would have believed it. But the feet were pale with black hairs on the knuckles of the toes. Jesse pushed himself off the wall so he could look up to see who they were attached to.

It was Nathan Ruskey. "Hey," Nathan said again. Maybe he didn't know any other words. Jesse hoped this was the case.

"Hey," Jesse said. "Sorry I punched you, I guess."

"It's cool." The feet paddled gently next to him. "Hey, I think you might be drunk. Do you need a ride home?"

Jesse tried to move away from where Nathan sat, forgetting he was in the pool. His heavy pants and the weight of the water made him stumble. Then the water caught him again as Jesse fell sideways, as if apologizing for putting him off balance in the first place. "With you? Are you kidding?"

"No," Nathan said. "I want to make sure you get home okay."

"Now you care about people getting home okay? Didn't they take away your license? Or didn't it matter, because you're Nathan Ruskey."

"What does that mean?" Jesse didn't say anything. "Listen," Nathan said. "I know it was my fault, even if people are telling me it wasn't." His voice sounded like someone had scratched it out of his throat; it sounded almost like the boy meant it.

"You drove into a fucking tree and killed my best friend," Jesse said. "What part of that is not your fault?" The last word rose up as Jesse's voice broke. People at the party still seemed not to see him, but they shifted like leaves in a light wind.

"Me?" Nathan said. He pulled his feet out of the water, rolled his pant legs back down. "I wasn't the one who was driving."

"You—what?" There was a flash in the distance. A thunderstorm? Headlights? An epic transfer of forgotten power?

On the edge of the pool, Nathan curled into himself. He tried to set his head on his bent knees and then jerked back, pressing a hand on his face. There was already a spreading bruise. At any other moment Jesse would be thrilled he caused that kind of damage. "She said that she was the most sober of all of us, and she took the keys out of my hand. I didn't know," Nathan said. His forehead went down against his knees now. "No one told me," Nathan said into his own body, and Jesse had to lean toward him to hear. "I woke up and there were lights everywhere and they told me my friend was dead. We weren't even friends," he said. "That's what I feel worst about. I hardly knew her." There was a horrible squelching sound: Nathan Ruskey was crying.

Jesse looked around, everywhere, anywhere else. Lia sat on the end of the diving board, the edges of her cape pulled around her shoulders. She chewed her lip, shrugged in the way that Jesse knew meant she was uncomfortable. She huddled deeper into the cape and Jesse recognized it now: her old baby quilt.

"I wanted to drive," she said. "And that car. That car is amazing, Jess. It's a Miata convertible, his mom gave it to him after he won the Junior Nationals in the IM." Lia stood up on the board, bounced once, and launched herself in their direction. She glided down on the side of the pool and crouched catlike near Nathan Ruskey. "I'm sorry about the car, Nate," she said. Nathan didn't hear, didn't even move.

"Your cape," Jesse said. He pulled himself out of the pool even though his clothes and the water drag back at him, urging him to stay. He sat next to Lia and pulled at the knot tied at her throat that was keeping her quilt in place. Jesse spread the quilt out and wrapped it around her, tucking it around her feet like she always used to do.

"I don't know, Jess," she said, finally. "I don't know how this works."

The two of them sat there for a long time at the side of the pool, the party noise rising and falling over itself like tides on a planet with two warring moons. At some point Nathan Ruskey curled up on his side and fell asleep. "Do you think I gave him a concussion? I should wake him up and get him talking," Jesse said. "Do you think anyone's wondering why I'm sitting over here with Nathan Ruskey?"

"No," Lia said. "You didn't give him a concussion. And they're not. They're not thinking about you at all." He wondered whether she was making fun of him, but this time she reached her arm out and put it around his back. He wasn't sure if it was the weight of her arm that he felt or the baby powder scent of the quilt, or the smell of the oranges—all those oranges—but she was there. She was real.

After a while, the smell of her was replaced by the chlorine from the pool and the water that had soaked his clothes. Jesse looked around. Lia was standing on top of the house again, at the very tip of the chimney, her boots almost too wide to fit. She stuck her lower lip out and blew up at her bangs to feather them off her face. It was a move that never really worked while she was alive, and it didn't work now. She pushed her hair out of the way with her hands. The strands stayed behind her ears for a moment before falling forward again. "You'd think at least I could have perfect hair now that I'm a superhero," she said. "Maybe I can ask the League what product they use. There might be something special."

This was the same line that would make it into the movie, the one that got maybe the best laughs, although Jesse only heard about that from others because he couldn't watch his own movie. Filming the movie had been fine—there were so many people and cranes and computers and it was all broken up into scenes and bits of scenes. But Jesse couldn't watch it once it was all together: beginning, middle, end. Because then Lia would get an arc, with failures, triumphs, and a resolution, the kind she was never allowed to have in real life. All he knew is that he would never quite understand what happened with Lia. For the movie, he made up how it ended in a way that left everyone feeling good.

The movie got all kinds of attention. Fans loved it, critics loved it. Even people who hated it, they hated it so colorfully that their online screeds only added to the movie's appeal. People asked him in the first round of publicity about his connection to the story. But the one time he said what really happened—*I had a friend who wanted to fly but she never felt like a superhero*—there must have been something about how he said it that makes his handlers hustle him into the next room. Somehow it never appeared in print, and the journalist who heard him say this was now a consulting writer on the studio's next project.

Mr. Boniface wrote him a note saying Lia would have loved it, too. He was still running the market, juicing oranges and taking breaks on the back dock to sit on a milkcrate and read the paper. Lia's sister Katy had been supportive even before that, talking up his movies on social media, even that terrible zombie one that he made in grad school. Jesse sent her passes, invited her to premieres, and he would see her in the distance through a kaleidoscope of colored gowns. They never seemed to find each other in the crowd.

Once the movie went to streaming, Jesse went home to Sacramento. At first, his parents treated him like an exchange student at lunch, using slow, vague words instead of proper nouns—your job, the place where you live, some of the people you work with. Then they opened a bottle of wine and his dad asked whether it was true that movie stars demanded particular brands of toilet paper or granola with all the raisins picked out by hand. His mother teased Jesse about his hair, which he started to shave once it was clear he was going bald. "I'll knit you some hats," she said, her teeth rosy with the wine. Jesse found this, suddenly and unexpectedly, endearing.

After lunch he walked through the afternoon heat to get more wine. The Bonifaces' market had expanded—there were travel coffee cups in sleek stainless steel, designer hand towels, an entire wall of wines by appellation. Jesse wandered the aisles with two bottles in his hand.

When he wandered around a display that paired artichokes with tiny artichoke-like succulents in handmade pots, he came face-to-face with Mrs. Boniface. "It's so good to see you," Jesse said. It was the first thing that came into his head, and it was true, and once it came out he knew it was the wrong thing to say. He held out the wine. "It's for my parents."

"I bet they're happy you're here, Jesse," she said. She wore glasses now, a green apron. He blinked: her face seemed almost Cubist, the expression shifting as an overhead fan threw shadow and light down on them. "I have to get something from the back. Excuse me," she said, wiping her hands on her apron as she turned and walked away. Jesse stood there for long minutes in the stop motion light of the fan before he realized she wasn't going to return.

Outside his parents' house, he set the wine down on the porch and sent a text to Katy. *I saw your mom at the store*, he wrote. *I think she ghosted me.* His phone showed her typing, and then the typing stopped. He tapped out another message: *I thought everything was ok?*

Yeah. Katy wrote back immediately. *I think she's missing Lia. Something I did?*

LOL. Make a movie about her. Another pause. *Mom says she wasn't a hero. She was just a girl. She just wanted Lia to have a chance to be a regular girl. She doesn't like people seeing her as a symbol of something.*

He started typing—*the beginning, that's how it really happened*—and then he deleted it. He was not sure whether he believed it himself anymore, not after all the stage sets and the stunt wires and the fans blowing in to make hair and capes flutter like they were actually in flight.

Katy again: *It's ok Jesse. She was my hero.* Just as this landed somewhere behind his rib cage—paired stripes of relief and despair—she wrote that her train was going into the tunnel, she'd try him later.

After a while Jesse took the wine inside and set it on the kitchen counter. His parents were napping at the back of the cool house. He sat on the sofa in the living room, where heavy curtains closed out the bright day outside, making it dark as the inside of a movie theater after everyone has gone home.

The ending scenes of Jesse's own movie showed the two main characters, boy and superhero, setting off together into the night. The super girl had learned to use her powers. The boy was always one step behind. It was the perfect ending, the producers said, to launch a sequel.

What really happened that night was that he stopped watching. That night at the party he had turned toward Lia to say something about her hair—something that would make her laugh. But when he opened his mouth it felt like he had an egg inside it. If he said anything, the egg would break, and he would spend the rest of his life cleaning the yolk off the world.

Instead, he had leaned over and shaken Nathan Ruskey by the shoulder. When Nathan roused himself, Jesse slid his arm around the taller boy's back and helped him up. He and Nathan Ruskey leaned against each other on their way out of the party. Jesse's invisibility cloak of nobody-ness covered both of them as they walked along the

Astroturf and out through a side gate. Somewhere behind him, air molecules ripped apart in a way that meant Lia had left the roof, her body traveling quickly. Jesse didn't turn around, even though later he realized that all he should have wanted was to see Lia fly.

That's what she'd wanted—she'd wanted to fly, hadn't she? He hadn't really been paying attention that day in the treehouse, when she tied the friendship bracelet to his wrist. He was thinking about being fast like Flash, fast enough to turn back time, maybe fast enough to separate his molecules from each other, to turn himself into something that people would notice, that wouldn't be so weak, that would stop his lungs from squeezing every time he moved faster than a jog. Lia's fingers, her nails covered in splashes of sparkle polish, flicked around his nine-year-old wrist. "You're supposed to wear this until it falls off," she said. "You shower with it, you sleep with it, you do everything with it."

"Gross," he said.

"Not gross. You make a wish now and then when it falls off, your wish comes true."

"You've got a lot of wishes," he said, looking at her skinny arm, rainbow bracelets halfway to her elbow.

She nodded, seriously. "None of them are to be a superhero, though."

"What are they, then?"

Then Lia's sister Katy came up the ladder into the treehouse, howling about how it wasn't fair that they could be here and she couldn't, and they slid away from her down the ladder to Jesse's house.

Jesse wore his bracelet for months, and he didn't remember it falling off. Even now, he could feel the blank spot on his wrist where the bracelet should have been, and he would never be able to run fast enough to go back in time, to find out where he lost it.

Suddenly, the empty dark of the living room felt unbearable. Jesse pushed himself off the couch and made his way to the backyard. Distant engines hummed along Land Park Drive, which had gotten busier in the twenty years since he lived here. There was a low buzz, too, which sounded like electricity but was really some summer-drunk insect. The ladder to the treehouse in his memory was towering. Now, it only took two steps up and he was inside again, where everything was at once smaller and larger than it had ever been.

The trapdoor on the far side, Lia's side, was open. Jesse leaned his head through to look into the Bonifaces' backyard. A piece of fabric hung from a branch just beneath him. The fabric rippled in the slight breeze. The rest of the air around Jesse went still. He would know it anywhere, even if he hadn't spent weeks with the prop department trying to re-create it: Lia's blanket, with two corners crumpled, as if someone had tied it together to form a cape.

The fabric looked no different than it had twenty years ago—old as it was then, but no older. Not faded as it would have been if it had been here in the sun this whole time.

He did what he always did now when he was uncertain of how to proceed: he reached for his phone. Lia never had a phone of her own. Jesse sat at the edge of the trap door, his grown-up feet dangling down into space, and opened up a new text screen.

I'm sorry, he wrote.

I miss you, he wrote.

I wish you had just been a girl, too. You were right about Nathan Ruskey. He was a pretty good guy. Better than me. Jesse pressed send. A series of red exclamation mark appeared, alerting him that he'd forgotten to enter a person from his contacts as the recipient. He hit the send button again. Nothing happened.

What did you wish for, with all of those wishes? he typed, and then deleted it. Whatever it was, he should have known the answer.

Jesse set down his phone and leaned out of the trapdoor of the treehouse to untie the blanket. Once it was in his hands he pulled himself back inside and bunched the fabric up to his face. Oranges, the metal-scent of a gathering storm. He wrapped the blanket around his legs, even though once he'd tucked it under his feet, the blanket only reached his shins. His phone flashed on. *I know*, a message said, and then it disappeared.

SHOELESS

WHEN THE MOTHER went outside to get the paper on Sunday morning, she saw that the shoes were gone. Not just a single pair. All of them. The flip-flops her husband wore to water the plants that the mother planted and then neglected. Her husband's work boots and his motorcycle boots. Her own running shoes, the old pair and the new pair. The sensible closed-toed shoes she wore to the lab.

The kids' shoes were gone, too. There were so many of them— there had been, anyway. Sneakers and soccer cleats, plastic clogs riddled with holes like Swiss cheese, a hand-me-down set of penny loafers with one penny in the slot of the right shoe. There had been cowboy boots with tiny lights that illuminated with each step. Water shoes and high tops and jelly sandals. Their front porch usually looked like the shoe section at the thrift store, which is where many of the shoes came from in the first place. She had four of them— children, that is—and their feet refused to stop growing, along with the rest of them, so there was no use getting anything new. The mother knew that was the idea with kids, that they grew.

She called back into the house. No one answered. Over her shoulder, her children slumped in various states of wakefulness at the long table. "Hey! I'm serious. Where are the shoes?"

Her oldest son unpeeled his eyes from one of the four screens at the table, each showing a different cartoon. He came and peered over her shoulder. He could look over her shoulder now, he was that tall. "Huh," he said. "I thought you were joking."

Her husband came down the hallway, rubbing his wet hair with a towel. With his hair spiked up like that, he looked like one of the boys. She wished she had known him as a boy, although if he'd known her as a girl, this whole moment would not be possible. As a girl, he would have found her strange—she had only liked being around people who were very young or very old, because they felt calm and understanding. When she first met her husband, he had the same quality: a serenity and good humor and reasonableness that seemed impossible to disturb.

Now, he looked over her shoulder, too. "Huh," he said, just like his son. "The shoes are gone."

The previous autumn, the family had visited Japan. The mother had been buzzy with pride as the children sat carefully on the step of their rented apartment and slipped off their shoes, unbidden, and set them on the genkan with the toes pointed out. At the end of their stay, their host had complimented them on how respectful the children were. The mother had laughed and then closed her mouth around the laugh and sneezed instead, which sent an ache across her lower belly that stopped the laugh all together.

Once they came home from Japan, her children started leaving their shoes on the front porch, one pair next to the other in a long line like they were ready to set off to join a parade. The careful arrangement of shoes only lasted for a few days. The shoes instead accumulated in a jangly pile, as if they could be used to start a small fire. This was her doing, too. The mother was always coming and going to a school or a grocery store, a soccer practice or a warehouse with bruised fruit, and then off to another grocery store, getting the things she'd forgotten at the first one. Once the mother got home, she would shuck off each shoe by stepping on the heel and kicking it backward, out of the doorway.

Still, the shoes stayed outside, and the house did seem cleaner. But maybe it wasn't really the shoes. Their old dog had died that autumn while they were in Japan, and so there was less dog hair, anyway, less everything.

It was spring now, and the shoes were gone. The shoes, the shoes. Where were the shoes now?

Maybe her husband had cleaned up again. The mother wished she was more like him, that she had cleaning binges. Cleaning made her angry and resentful, although she also cleaned the best when she was feeling angry and resentful. She came inside to look in the bottom of her closet, where she used to keep her shoes before they starting living respectfully outside. No shoes, still: the bottom of the mother's closet looked like a toothless mouth.

The mother climbed up into the attic, where they put everything that didn't have a place, including shoes. She ducked underneath the rafters and stepped carefully around the water heater to find the boxes where they kept clothes that they were saving for another child to grow into them. But while there were long johns and warm jackets and woolen hats, there were no seldom-used snow boots. There was no carton of dress shoes that lingered there, just in case someone asked the family to a wedding or a bar mitzvah, or if they needed to appear—she hoped not—in court or at a funeral. There was no back-up box of shoes saved for the next baby, because there would be no next baby. She could not find the booties her grandmother had knitted for their very first baby. The booties were pale green and had fluffy tassels the size of ping pong balls on the ends. Even though the mother had lost field trip permission slips and water bottles and her wallet and, once, two entire shipping containers of peaches, she'd managed to keep the booties for all these years. At least until now.

In the attic, she started to cry. Silently, the mother thought. Then she heard her husband call up the attic stairs: "What's wrong, sugar?" He had a sixth sense for tears. Not that hers made any sense. She could cry for shoes, but if anything truly sad happened, her tear ducts seemed to go dormant. The mother had loved her grandmother so much, could still feel the cool of her cheek and the scent of roses if she thought of it, but at her grandmother's funeral the mother couldn't make her face go the right way, and her own mother had told her to go sit in the back if she couldn't wipe that smirk off her face. Her own mother had no problem crying over the things that were worth crying about.

In the attic, she pressed at the inner corners of her eyes with her thumb and forefinger. Now you decide to work, she said to her tear ducts. This was not an emergency, it was just strange. She should be able to deal with strange by now.

"What's that?" her husband called again. His head popped up through the opening in the attic.

She looked away into a shoeless box. "Did you get rid of the hand-me-down box with the shoes? I can't seem to find it anywhere." The mother couldn't control her face, but she could make her voice sound like anyone she wanted. Now she made it sound like the most cheerful worker at an ice-cream store. "This is a puzzle, isn't it?"

Her husband turned back down the ladder. "This isn't funny anymore, you animals," he called down to the kids. "Where did you hide the shoes?"

Of course: the children had taken them. Her husband always thought of the straightforward solutions that she missed. The twins had once hidden a babysitter's shoes in an attempt to say that they didn't like having a babysitter, although the effect had been that the sitter had to stay twenty minutes longer while she and the parents searched the house for a pair of olive suede Birkenstocks, size 46. The mother had paid the sitter overtime for the shoe hunt. Until that moment, the mother had not realized what large feet the babysitter had.

When she came down the ladder, shoeless, the children looked as baffled as her husband. Then they all looked at each other—the oldest boy, the twin girls in the middle, and then the youngest, also a boy. "If we don't have shoes, we don't have to go to school," the youngest said.

"Now, wait a minute—" her husband said, but they had already started dancing around the living room, the twins hopping up onto the couch and using it as a trampoline.

"But you like school," the mother said.

Her youngest stopped and looked at her. "Is today a holiday where people make shoes disappear?" After they'd come back from Japan, she'd started celebrating minor holidays as a way to break up the dullness that seemed to settle on her. There were so many holidays: French Toast Day, National Wear a Tie Day, Sneak Some Zucchini onto the Neighbor's Porch Day.

"I don't think so," the mother said. She'd forgotten to look up what that day was.

"It's National Blueberry Muffin Day," the oldest said, tapping away at a screen. "Can we make muffins?"

"I'll have to go to the store," she said. She looked down at her feet.

"Oh," he said. "What about basketball practice?"

The twins had stopped bouncing. "What about school? We actually do like school, we just wanted to jump on the couch." The youngest came and held her hand: he did not like school. She squeezed his hand.

"Let's not panic, people," her husband said. He looked at her. "Do you want to go for a run? You'll feel more like yourself. You know, more happy."

She did, this was exactly the time she went for a run, when everything was too much. While she was gone, he would solve this problem for her, the problem of the shoes. He was always solving the problems for her that she couldn't solve. She had given up on solving. The mother opened the front door before remembering that the shoes were still gone. Behind her, she could hear her youngest child saying to her, "You're always happy anyway, aren't you?"

"I am," she said, and closed the door. As she did, she understood that not even a run could help her feel more like herself—she hadn't known who that was in years.

Her bare right foot on the accelerator, the mother drove downtown, looking for shoe stores. The twins came with her. They sat in the back seat, each of them holding an arm out of a side window. "Let's fly!" they told her, so the mother made jet noises as they circled the blocks. She imagined them banking to the left, then barrel rolling to escape an oncoming garbage truck.

"Scouts, tell me when you get line-of-sight on Foot Locker." There was a coffee and pastries shop where Foot Locker used to be. There was a coffee and doughnut shop where the mom-and-pop shoestore used to be, the one where she went as a child, where they tied a helium balloon to her wrist as her mother bought her white sneakers with red stripes. The other department store had an enormous **FOR LEASE** sign on it, and also a sign that it was being converted in to a roller rink and arcade with a coffee shop. Until this moment, the mother had loved coffee.

The girls hung out the window and begged her to stop.

The mother made her voice deep and gruff, the flight commander. "Today's mission is shoes."

"Oh, Mom," the curly-haired twin said. She had grown up in the space of two minutes; she picked at her sparkly nails while her sister stuck her arm back out the window and tried to fly this plane with one wing. "Everyone gets shoes online these days, don't you know?"

"Mission aborted," the mother said, and turned the car for home. On second thought, maybe she would get a coffee. If they went to the drive-through, no one would notice their naked feet.

When they got home, the mother went online. Her daughter had been right: there they were, shoes in every size and color, shoes that could be delivered to her home by tomorrow. She had tried not to buy things online, but now it seemed like a rare form of magic, making disappearing shoes reappear in 24 hours, all with free shipping.

This time, she would go basic. Another piece of magic: the chance to simplify. She chose a pair of clogs for herself for work, some plain lace-up shoes for her husband, sneakers for each of the kids in colors that would hide the dirt. She went to check out. Her cart was empty.

The mother went back to the beginning, picking out the same pair for each of them. Once again, she clicked the button for her cart, but no shoes showed up. Then she started adding wild pairs, leopard print knee-highs and vegan men's platform ankle boots. Nothing seemed to take—the cart sloughed each pair off to somewhere unknowable. She imagined a warehouse somewhere, the leopard print knee-highs and platform ankle boots vanishing from their shoeboxes in a puff of smoke. When she thought of the empty boxes, she felt lonely. Her youngest child came to lean his head against her shoulder. "Don't get me flip flops," he said. "I hate how they feel between my toes."

"I won't," she said. "I promise."

The mother called a neighbor who had slightly older children and asked whether she had any hand-me-downs. "You know how it is, suddenly I can't seem to find anything that fits." She didn't mention that she couldn't find anything at all.

There was a pause. Then the neighbor said of course, she had just the thing. She'd be right over.

The neighbor arrived with a muffin tin. "Oh, I must have mumbled," said the mother, whose children sometimes covered their ears because her voice was too full of sunshine in the mornings. "I meant shoes. Silly me." The neighbor tilted her head to one side, charming and confused.

"Of course!" the neighbor said at last. "I forgot those little paper cups. So sorry, I'll be right back."

The neighbor returned with the muffin wrappers. She was a red-headed woman whose head looked like an egg someone had painted a face on. The mother thanked her. "It's National Blueberry Muffin Day, you know. You really saved the day," the mother said. Her own smile also felt painted on, but at least it was there.

"Oh, I know," the neighbor said. "I made mine last night. But you have a lot going on." She waved at the mother's house, including the front porch, where there still weren't any shoes. The mother wondered whether both of their faces would crack with all that smiling.

After the neighbor went back to her house, the mother watched people walking their dogs down the street. They all had shoes—not the dogs, the people. She and her husband once got tiny shoes for their dog, when they used to take the dog hiking in the mountains and the granite tore at his paws. People told her she treated that dog like a baby. She did. What was wrong with giving small creatures all of your love? It was wrong because you were left with nothing when they left you, a small mean voice inside her said. Her husband had always been good about telling that mean voice to go away. Even that problem, he could solve.

Before they'd left for Japan, she hadn't said goodbye to the dog as she usually did, three scratches under the chin and a kiss on the head. In truth, it was the first time she hadn't worried about the dog, going away—he was old, but in the days before they left, he seemed happier than ever, curled up next to the side of her bed at night, following her from room to room until she sat down on the couch and stayed. She told herself that she was doing it for the dog, so he wouldn't have to get up again. Since no one was watching, she let him up on the couch and they had both fallen asleep, nestled against each other. When she woke, she couldn't remember what day it was, or even what year, and then she remembered that those kind of naps—the ones that took everything from her, left her groggy and shaken—had always happened to her when she was pregnant. She couldn't possibly be pregnant, though—her husband had solved that one. They had both agreed: no more children. He'd gotten a vasectomy.

And yet, here she was, unsolved. After the first wave of terror, she felt giddy. She decided she wasn't going to tell anyone yet. They were just about to go to Japan, after all. And she'd already learned that people stopped being excited for her. When she had the baby after the twins, people would give her a look that said, isn't it enough already?

When Monday came, they all needed to go back to the places they were supposed to be, shoes or no shoes. Her husband said that he'd take the kids in through the school's front office and talk with the vice-principal, who seemed to have taken a shine to him.

The vice-principal did not like the mother, who, a few times over the past months, felt a sharp wind roll through her chest that made her pick up the phone and call the school office to say that she was worried about one of her children, would they go check? The children were fine, always fine. She did not tell her children about these calls. She did not tell her husband, either. Sometimes she still called the school office, but she hung up when the secretary answered. This seemed to make the wind settle down until she went to pick the children up again.

Today her husband called her while she drove to the lab, the rubber stripes of the accelerator rippling underneath her toes. "It's no problem," he said.

"What did they say?"

"They went into the lost and found to see if they could find shoes for them, but there wasn't anything. So they said they could just go to class today. They don't seem to have a specific rule against it." Her husband was a lawyer. If there was a rule, he would find a loophole. That was what she had planned to say when she told him about the baby: the baby was the loophole. But she never did have to tell him. Now on the phone, he was as calm as always. "Let's just carry on as usual," he said. "I'm sure this will work itself out." He said that he loved her and hung up before her voice could squeeze itself into the shape of agreeing he was right.

At her office, the mother put on her white coat and her safety glasses and stepped into the lab where she was working on peaches. She had been here for years, making substances that protected fruit from bruising when it was transported. At first, she worked with easier fruits, like thick-skinned grapefruits and oranges. Now she supervised the younger lab techs, she developed safety protocols, and she was synthesizing a compound specific to peaches, which were especially fragile.

Usually no one came in her lab, but today her supervisor brought in a group of potential investors on a tour of the facilities. The investors looked at the long benches and the test tubes and the humming centrifuge. The supervisor looked down at her feet.

She showed the investors the rows of peaches that she'd painted with her compound and then dropped on the laboratory floor. The skin of the peaches was pink and tender. She then showed the investors the untreated peaches, which looked like they had been in a boxing match. The investors smiled. Her supervisor did not smile.

An hour later, he called the mother into his office. "You were the one who developed the safety protocols," he said.

She tried to tell him about the shoes, but it was as if he didn't hear. "I suppose you can do inventory on the cold storage this week while we figure out next steps," he said. But how could there be any next steps without next shoes to take them in?

She still had to make dinner.

When she got home, the only thing on the porch was a spiderweb. The spider, pale with dark markings along its abdomen, zigzagged across a part of its web that had come apart. The spider's legs twitched, frantic in its repair. The spider, the mother thought, would need so many shoes. There was something caught in its web, she realized. A tiny piece of silver hair, left behind by the dog.

In Japan, she was the one who'd known about the dog first. She had a jet-lagged dream their first night about soft silver fur and a beach with shining pebbles and a ball, endlessly thrown. Her own grandmother had been there, too. In the dream, there was a small fluttering in the palm of her hand, like a trapped moth, and in the dream this fluttering made perfect sense, although she would not remember it until later. She had woken up to three messages from the vet—first asking for her permission, then telling her that the dog had been in such distress that the vet had made a decision without her—and the palm of her hand slipped under her bra, which she had forgotten to take off.

Still, they had been happy. They had visited all the places the children wanted to, and found it all delightful: the comic book museum, the toy store, the statue of patient Hachiko, the dog that waited for his person every day at the subway entrance. Then his person, a professor, had a cerebral hemorrhage while in the middle of a lecture. Hachiko continued to wait. Her oldest son had read them all this from the guidebook: the dog came to the station every day for more than nine years. The children found a dog toy at a nearby store and left it as an offering by the statue, in honor of their own dog.

A few days later, the mother started leaving her own offerings of blood in the lovely Japanese toilets. (The warm seats! The various spray directions and water temperatures! The charming music that played so no one could hear you crying about something that was just a loophole!) They were all so *happy*. The mother decided, then, that the lost baby didn't even bear mentioning. Look, she could solve a problem, too.

After their first day at school, the children seemed to think that not having shoes was a positive turn of events. They found that running in the grass barefoot during PE felt like flying. They scaled the playground slides like geckos. They attended soccer practice and their footwork blossomed, but they didn't have to play in the games on the weekends, where cleats were required. Instead, the children wandered the neighborhood streets for hours, their bare soles becoming immune to the radiant heat of the sidewalk.

The mother's soles did not adapt. Neither did her boss. She kept trying to explain, but from the way her boss's face looked and the things he said, the only thing he heard was that she refused to wear shoes. (*But she wanted to! She wanted to! She just couldn't find them.*) A month later, she left the lab with a cardboard box of her things, along with a water bottle and fleece jacket displaying the company's logo: a smiling apple, untouched by any injury the world could offer.

During the day, now, the mother cleaned. There were no more traces of dog hair. She was no longer angry or resentful when she cleaned, she was just not sure of anything else she could do. The mother wished she had thought to fill up the water bottle with her peach-protecting compound on the way out. She could rub it all over her body. Even though her house was now the cleanest it had ever been, everything hurt, not just her feet, but everything.

The only thing that calmed her was washing her children's feet each night. Their feet returned home each day soaked in dirt, having found the muddiest patches of grass. The mother took the washcloth and held their strong ankles in her hands, wiping firmly enough so that they were not tickled, gently enough so that they didn't feel any pain.

One afternoon, they went to a playground at the far side of town which held enormous moving sculptures that the children could climb, surrounded by sand. The mother sat at a picnic table at the side of the playground. Soon, her youngest came to sit next to her. Once, he didn't like the feeling of sand in his shoes. Now he didn't like the feeling of the sand between his toes. "I would like it if the sand were made of shoes and our feet were made of sand," he said. "Then everything would be all right."

That night, as she wiped his feet, she tried to imagine what feet would be like if they were sand. While she cleaned one of his feet, his other foot felt asleep. "There's still sand in my toes!" he cried. He could not stop crying until after she turned out the bedroom lights, long after the feeling must have returned.

She sat on the couch, the house so clean around her that she could not help but notice the terrible emptiness surrounding everything, even her sleeping children, who could be swallowed by the same emptiness at any minute. Her whole body felt like it was made of sand. Everything could crumble. "Tell me what's wrong," her husband said. He brought her a cup of tea.

"You always know how to help," the mother said.

"I wish that were true," her husband said. At the school the other day, as she waited for her children in a skirt so long that no one could see her toes, she heard the other mothers talking about Hot Barefoot Dad. She tripped over her skirt as she moved away. No one called her Hot Barefoot Mom. No one called her much of anything. How could they, when she wasn't sure what to call herself anymore? It was just her and her feet, fragile as unprotected fruit.

One evening—the house clean, the children's feet washed and in their beds, the grown-ups' bare feet in their own bed—she told him that sometimes she fantasized about tackling someone at the grocery store and pulling off their shoes. "I know it wouldn't work," she said. "I'm sure something would happen, like the shoes wouldn't come off, or they would disappear as soon as I put them on. But still. Do you ever think like that?"

The husband looked down at his toes and wiggled them. "I think we should go to Japan."

"Why?" Then she remembered what she'd told him. "Do you think they'll have shoes there?"

He reached over and put a hand on the side of her face. "It's the last time I remember that you were happy."

"I am happy," she said, and she rolled over to turn off the light. "I am," she whispered to the darkness.

Last time when they'd visited, they'd been given slippers at every place they'd stayed. They received so many slippers that they'd taken them home as gifts.

This time, when they arrived, their host gave them paper fans. "They are for our returning guests," said the host, who walked them to their room. "Thank you for coming back again."

"We were really happy here," the mother said.

The host opened the door to their room and waited for them to step inside. Then he began to wave his hands. "You must," he said, drawing small circles with his hands at the ground. He seemed to have lost what he wanted to say, though it was clearly important. "Take off. Your shoes." He said it loudly, as if she did not understand.

"I can't take off my feet," the mother said.

"Maybe pull?" the host said. He mimed tugging at his heels. "Pull," he said again, drawing out the word.

"I can't," the mother said. "They're attached to me."

"Of course we can do that," her husband said, sitting down on the low step and reaching for his own heel. "Of course we can." The children sat down next to their father, looking earnestly at their own feet.

Her children's feet. Look at their feet! Their feet were tough and wiry now, with toes that could grip onto tree branches and climb ladders. Oh, their toes! The oldest one's rounded toes, which looked like his father's, who right now was sitting there with his rolled-up trousers, the black hair spiking out around his ankles. The twins, one with blue toenail polish, one with green, each like a tiny drop of tropical water on their toes. And the little one, his long narrow toes just as she remembered her grandmother's feet, which were elegant and surprising for a woman whose body had been rounded with love. The mother remembered each of her children't feet when they were babies, how soft and wrinkled they were, how she would cradle their feet in her hands. How she felt, at that long-ago moment, so clear in what she was doing, like she would never forget anything, never lose anything, that she had everything she needed.

The host watched her. "It must be hard to keep track of things, with so many children," he said.

What could she say, that he was right? That she should not have been so greedy as to want more? One more tiny pair of feet to keep track of. She looked down at her own feet so that he would not see her face. She was having trouble breathing, her lungs like raisins, like they'd always felt when something truly awful had happened but that tears were too small to wash it away.

Down below her, her own toes gripped the edge of the wooden entryway. As if they noticed she was watching, her toes flexed and stretched. How could she not have noticed them all along? She would not take off her feet, she had lost enough already.

"I'm sorry," she said. "I'm sorry, I'm sorry." The man started to murmur something, but she was not apologizing to the man. "Come on," she said to the children, to her husband.

For once, they did not hesitate. All their feet followed hers. Their feet took them to the train station, where yellow stencils of footprints marked the line where people should wait for the train. The family stood on the outlines and waited until the train came.

On board, their bodies swayed with the movement of the train. Her oldest bumped against her, as he used to do when he was little, and this time he leaned into her. Her feet held them both in place, even when the train jerked to a stop at each station. Her feet held them both up all the way until the doors open at the end of the line. Outside the station there was a small sign with an arrow that points to a wave and a beach umbrella. She began to run.

She heard laughter behind her. She thought about the laughter, years ago, when she and her husband had travelled and lost and found themselves in unlikely places. They tried out new words with laughing children or mixed up the words for garlic and fish head, or held out maps upside down to strangers for help. All of their mistakes seemed to be promising. There was never too much to keep track of, that they would always be able to fumble along, and they wouldn't lose anyone along the way.

Now the pavement cooled under her soles. Then her strong feet felt the wide planks of a boardwalk, and then the sand.

At the edge of the sea there was a line of shoes. The toes all pointed toward the water, as if left by someone who had walked into the ocean. There were large rain boots and medium-sized flip flops and sneakers and Mary Janes and even, improbably, a pair of ice skates, the blades sparkling in the sun. The line seemed to go on down the beach forever. If the mother went far enough, she understood she would find a small pair of booties. If she went far enough, she would maybe find everything she had ever lost. She would be able to keep track of everything.

Then the children came behind her, their shining faces, their dirty feet still attached to them. "You're fast, Mom," her oldest said. And in the far distance, walking, then jogging, was her husband. When he reached her, he took her hand and held it softly enough to imagine something alive in the space between their cupped palms. "Did you know that you can't actually take off your feet? They're attached to you," he said. She brought his hand to her chest. If she tried to find everything she has lost, she would miss all of this.

"Look, mama," the youngest one said. "The beach is made of shoes. Are our feet made of sand?" Her feet did feel like they were tingling, like they were coming to life after having been asleep for a long time. She knew that if they tried to step into any one of these pairs of shoes that waited on the beach, the shoes would fit. They would not disappear. But she didn't want to do it, not quite yet. Instead she found a break in the long line of shoes and walked past them into the sea.

Her family followed. They all bobbed next to each other in the water, the shoes waiting for them on the shore. "What if it was World Swim in the Ocean Day?" the oldest one asked.

"It should be," the curly-haired twin said. "Or maybe it's National Hug Your Dog Day." They all floated there for a while. The mother thought about putting her arms around all that silvery fur, about burying her face in it. Her dog had never cared what her face looked like, only about the sound of her voice and a few precious words, like *walk* and *dinner* and *come* and *treat.*

"Mom, can we get ice cream soon?" the youngest one said.

The mother didn't answer. She lifted her toes out of the water so she could see them. There they were, bright and stubby and hers.

The quieter, straight-haired twin paddled over to the mother and floated next to her. "How come we never wash your feet, Mom?" she asked. While the twins usually looked only like sisters, here in the water they looked like two creatures made from the same body, which, the mother supposed, they were.

"It's hard to keep track of everything," she said.

ACKNOWLEDGMENTS

Thank you to the following journals for publishing these stories, and for all the work you do to support writers and artists.

"Star, Fish," *Terrain.org*
"Adult Swim," *Levee*
"Ripening," *PANK*
"The Coat," *District Lit*
"Slow Motion," *The Missouri Review*
"Golden Hour," *Prometheus Dreaming*
"St. Lucia Brings the Light," *Flash Fiction Magazine*
"Mr. October," *Storm Cellar*
"How to Capture Carbon," *Five South*
"Pie Tin," *Carve*

THANK YOU

To the team at What Books Press, for believing in these stories. To Rod Val Moore and Mona Houghton, for making them better. To ash good and Gronk, for making them beautiful.

To my beloved cloud makers—Ho-Ming So Denduangrudee, Louise Freeman, Noami Pines, Yurika Tamura—I feel so lucky that we found each other. I'm not sure that I'd be writing this without the magic of your support. Thank you to Sabrina Orah Mark for bringing us together and showing us that kindness adds the sparkle to writing, and to life.

To the editors who were champions of these stories in their earliest forms. Special thanks to Bridget Apfeld at *Carve*, Elizabeth Walztoni at *Five South*, Simmons Buntin at Terrain.org, and to Joy Castro, for shining your light on "Star, Fish."

To Lenka Clayton and Rachel Fallon for the ongoing Residency in Motherhood. To teachers and mentors through the years: Sister Maureen Viani, Ann Pancake, Justin Cronin, David Huddle, Katey Schultz, Sarah Selecky, Heidi Reimer, Sarah Freligh, and Abbigail Rosewood. To friends near and far who inspire me with their own creative pursuits, and who have always supported mine: Christie Aschwanden, Kathi Rivers Shannon, April Ayers Lawson, Shannon Cronin, Miranda Weiss, Marianne Moser, Viktoriya Filippova, Helen Fields. To D.J. Palladino for the home field advantage, and to independent bookstores in California and beyond.

To Steve Kettman, Sarah Ringler, and family for the restorative creative sanctuary at the Wellstone Center in the Redwoods. Thanks to Mathilde Hjertholm Nielsen, Daniel Escoto, and Sara Roahen for making it fun. Belated gratitude to the Vermont Studio Center (and the Muses!), the Anderson Center at Tower View, and to the very special Kettle River Residency for the long-ago introduction to the value of time spent writing and learning with artists and writers from around the world.

Time is a gift at home, too, and many wonderful people helped me find more of it so that I could work on these stories: Franny Higgins and family, Trina Diaz, Jessie Sexton, Annie Gupta, Megan Bright, Emily Ashlock, Denise Jaimes-Villanueva, Jayne Patterson, and the SBMS/DPHS carpool crews. And to Franny, again, for the pie and the love.

There aren't enough words to thank my dear family, but I'll keep trying. Thank you forever to the LaBerge girls: favorite sisters, storytellers, role models of both style and substance. To Sue, for making me a part of your own beautiful family. And to Chris, and to my boys. My loves. You are the helium in my heart balloon.

CAMERON WALKER is the author of *National Monuments of the U.S.A.* (a School Library Journal Best Book of the Year), and the essay collection *Points of Light*. Her short fiction and essays have won awards from Terrain.org and the American Society of Journalists & Authors. She lives in California with her family.

WHAT BOOKS PRESS

AN IMPRINT OF

THE GLASS TABLE

COLLECTIVE

LOS ANGELES

All WHAT BOOKS feature cover art by Los Angeles painter, printmaker, muralist, and theater and performance artist GRONK. A founding member of ASCO, Gronk collaborates with the LA and Santa Fe Operas and the Kronos Quartet. His work is found in the Corcoran, Smithsonian, LACMA, and Riverside Art Museum's Cheech Marin collection.

As a small, independent press, we urge our readers to support independent booksellers. This is easily done on our website by purchasing our books from Bookshop.org.

WHATBOOKSPRESS.COM

2019

Time Crunch
CATHY COLMAN
POEMS

Whole Night Through
L.I. HENLEY
POEMS

Echo Under Story
KATHERINE SILVER
NOVEL

Decoding Sparrows
MARIANO ZARO
POEMS

2018

Interrupted by the Sea
PAUL LIEBER
POEMS

The Headwaters of Nirvana
BILL MOHR
POEMS

2017

*Gary Oldman Is a Building
You Must Walk Through*
FORREST ROTH
NOVEL

Rhombus and Oval
JESSICA SEQUEIRA
STORIES

Imperfect Pastorals
GAIL WRONSKY
POEMS

2016

The Mysterious Islands
A.W. DEANNUNTIS
STORIES

*The "She" Series:
A Venice Correspondence*
HOLADAY MASON
& SARAH MACLAY
POEMS

Mirage Industries
CAROLIE PARKER
POEMS

2015

*The Balloon Containing
the Water Containing the
Narrative Begins Leaking*
RICH IVES
STORIES

*The Shortest Farewells
Are the Best*
CHUCK ROSENTHAL
& GAIL WRONSKY
LITERARY COLLAGE/PROSE POEMS

2014

It Looks Worse Than I Am
LAURIE BLAUNER
POEMS

They Become Her
REBBECCA BROWN
NOVEL

*The Final Death of Rock-and-
Roll
& Other Stories*
A.W. DEANNUNTIS
STORIES

Perfecta
PATTY SEYBURN
POEMS

2013

Brittle Star
ROD VAL MOORE
NOVEL

Sex Libris
JUDITH TAYLOR
POEMS

Start With A Small Guitar
LYNNE THOMPSON
POEMS

Tomorrow You'll Be One of Us
GAIL WRONSKY,
CHUCK ROSENTHAL
& GRONK
ART/LITERARY COLLAGE/POEMS

2012

*The Mermaid at the Americana
Arms Motel*
A.W. DEANNUNTIS
NOVEL

The Time of Quarantine
KATHARINE HAAKE
NOVEL

Frottage & Even As We Speak
MONA HOUGHTON
NOVELLAS

*West of Eden:
A Life in 21ˢᵗ Century Los Angeles*
CHUCK ROSENTHAL
MAGIC JOURNALISM

2010

Master Siger's Dream
A.W. DEANNUNTIS
NOVEL

Other Countries
RAMÓN GARCÍA
POEMS

A Giant Claw
GRONK
ESSAY BY GAIL WRONSKY
SPANISH TRANSLATION
BY ALICIA PARTNOY
ART

*Coyote O'Donohughe's
History of Texas*
CHUCK ROSENTHAL
NOVEL

So Quick Bright Things
GAIL WRONSKY
BILINGUAL, SPANISH TRANSLATION
BY ALICIA PARTNOY
POEMS

2009

*Bling & Fringe
(The L.A. Poems)*
MOLLY BENDALL &
GAIL WRONSKY
POEMS

April, May, and So On
FRANÇOIS CAMOIN
STORIES

One of Those Russian Novels
KEVIN CANTWELL
POEMS

*The Origin of Stars
& Other Stories*
KATHARINE HAAKE
STORIES

Lizard Dream
KAREN KEVORKIAN
POEMS

*Are We Not There Yet?
Travels in Nepal,
North India, and Bhutan*
CHUCK ROSENTHAL
MAGIC JOURNALISM

LOS ANGELES